knight watch gallery

KnightWatch Gallery

The Knightwatch Press Chapbook Collection

Black Shuck Books
www.blackshuckbooks.co.uk

First published in Great Britain in 2018 by
Black Shuck Books
Kent, UK

978-1-913038-29-8

the night just got darker

"We talked on, unmindful of the gathering shadows…"
The King in Yellow – Robert W. Chambers

Dedicated to Joel Lane
(1963-2013)

For a long time I have pondered the idea of what it really means to tell stories. After what happened, and certainly during the continuing aftermath, the very notion of storytelling has begun to take on a much more sinister tone. We're all part of a story – indeed, aren't we all the main character in the story of our own lives? But what if those stories aren't everything they're cracked up to be? What if all our stories are subject to the whim of a single overworked author? Writing and rewriting; working and reworking, just to hold back the darkness.

These thoughts plague me in the middle of the night, when I find it difficult to sleep. When the darkness seems thicker, denser than it should, and the house across the street seems somehow more than empty. Most nights I'll go to my study and stare at the window across the way – the place where it all began for me. There's never anyone sitting there, but I can remember so clearly a time when there was.

My thoughts are always dark at these moments, during those long nights.

Sometimes I can cast them off in the morning. Often they stay with me, darkening even the brightest of days.

~

I hate going to bed early. If I do, I'm usually unable to sleep peacefully for longer than a few hours at a time. Even as a child, I'd fight my parents' calls for me to go up to my room, staying up past my bedtime to watch something on television.

Early nights rarely agree with me; I have always been a creature of the late hours.

At some point during the night in question – in the long, quiet hours before dawn – I was sitting up in bed and staring at the greyish square of the window blind. It looked like a screen in the moment before moving pictures are projected onto its surface: bright, expectant, full of promise.

Darkness pressed in around me but I did not feel trapped; I felt poised at the edge of an experience. Somewhere outside, perhaps as close as a few streets away, a car exhaust backfired. A dog barked. A bottle smashed against brick or stone. I glanced over at my wife, Kath, but she was still sleeping. I leaned over, trying to hear if she was breathing, but I could not make out a sound. Resisting the urge to touch her, I watched the gentle rise and fall of her chest.

Minutes passed. Or was it just seconds? Kath moaned

in her sleep, turned over with her back to me. The moment – whatever it was – had been broken.

I shut my eyes, opened them again, and lay back down on the bed. It was no use. I couldn't sleep, not now that I was fully awake. My mind was racing but the thoughts were unclear. I knew the feeling well and often dreaded its arrival.

Rising slowly, so as not to disturb Kath, I slipped out of bed, left the room, and walked slowly along the landing. I was wearing only my boxer shorts – I rarely slept in anything else – but the heating had come on during the night so I wasn't cold. The study door was open. I walked in, shutting the door behind me, and sat down at my desk by the window. The desk lamp was still on – I must have forgotten to switch it off earlier – and there was a novel open in front of me: Treasure Island, an old favourite. I picked up the book and began to read.

Before long, I glanced up from the page and out of the window. The front garden was overgrown. The privet hedges needed a trim. Our lawn looked sad and tired in the unforgiving light of the street lamps. I allowed my gaze to roam, taking in the quiet street, the darkened houses. But in one house a light blazed from an upper floor window. From where I was sitting, I could see right into the room.

The man was there again, in the house opposite ours. He'd been there every night that week. I could see him through the open curtains. A small man, with thinning dark hair, sitting at a desk located in a similar position to the one in which I was seated. The house was but a few hundred yards away across the narrow street, so I could make out exactly what the man was doing: he was typing at a computer keyboard. Small spectacles with thin frames reflected meagre light. The man seemed to be concentrating furiously; the look on his face was intense. Every now and then one of his hands would come up and rub at his brow, as if pushing back an imaginary fringe of hair.

I'd never seen him prior to this week. This was a quiet neighbourhood, where most people tended to keep to themselves. We didn't chat with the neighbours; there was never any reason to call on them for a social visit or to complain. We lived like strangers, barely even aware of each other's existence.

I put down my book and watched the man. He was lost in his work. Even from that distance, I could see the immense concentration that gripped his entire body, making him sit rigid in his chair.

As I stared, the man glanced up, stopped typing, and smiled, as if he'd known all along that he was being watched. The smile, though, was far from a happy expression. It was filled with what I could only describe as grief, or perhaps longing.

It certainly did nothing for his drawn, gaunt features. Later, when I had occasion to think of the moment again, I decided that what I had seen in his smile was in fact a note of despair.

Unaccountably guilty, as if I'd been caught watching a woman undress, I felt myself blushing. Heat seared my cheeks. I blinked. Not knowing what else to do, I raised a hand and waved. The man in the window opposite took off his glasses, wiped them on a handkerchief, and then replaced them. He rubbed at his forehead in what I already thought of as his trademark gesture. Then he waved back, but slowly: a tiny, timid gesture in the night.

When he returned his attention to whatever he was writing, I felt lost for a moment, as if the late hour was about to swallow me up. I reached out and switched off the lamp, sat in the darkness for a little while longer, watching the man as he continued to work. His brow was knitted with concentration. He had eyes for nothing but the screen in front of him. I wondered what he was working on, what kind of task required such a high level of concentration.

After several more minutes, I left the room and went back to bed.

~

Kath was up before me the following morning. She pulled on her clothes and applied her makeup in front of the dressing table mirror as I incrementally entered the waking world. I wasn't sure at which point I'd managed to fall asleep, but it felt like I'd only shut my eyes five minutes ago.

Kath didn't speak to me; she ignored the fact that I was there, watching her through bleary eyes. I stared at her as she pulled on her trousers, admiring her long, slim legs. I felt an erection twitch into life beneath the duvet, but tried to ignore it. We hadn't made love for over a month; so long that I couldn't even pinpoint the last time we'd done so.

"See you tonight," she said as she rushed out of the room. I didn't hear her go down the stairs but I did hear the front door slam on her way out of the house. A sense of loss passed over me, as if I should be mourning something, but it only lasted for a couple of seconds before leaving me empty.

After staying there as long as I could, I finally got out of bed. Took a dump. Washed. Brushed my teeth. Ate a tasteless breakfast of toast and cereal. I switched on the television as I ate. Reports of street crime, corrupt politicians; a baby had been raped by an ageing pop star as its stoned mother watched. The news was depressing me but I couldn't summon the energy to switch it off, so I kept watching, stuffing bland cereal into my mouth.

The bus into town was packed, as always. The buildings outside the window transformed from residential homes to warehouses and offices. The grubby canal wound its way along the same route. I put in my earphones and tried to listen to some Leonard Cohen, but the man occupying the seat in front of me was a constant distraction. The pages of his huge broadsheet newspaper flapped like the wings of a bird of prey, constantly drawing my gaze. I got off the bus a stop before the one I needed, glad to be back out in the open air. For a moment, I thought about turning around and walking home, calling in sick when I got there, and spending the day reading, watching TV, or listening to music.

But I did none of that. I went to work, sat at my desk, and crunched data for eight hours, wishing that I had the nerve to pack it in and do something else.

That evening I was home before Kath. She sent me a text message saying that she was staying out for a drink with her workmates and they might go for a curry later.

I'd not met any of them before. She hadn't even spoken to me of them. It occurred to me then that we led separate lives, neither of which intersected at any point. Even the space we shared in our home was filled with compartments, and we passed by each other all the time without really connecting in any substantial way.

I made myself a bowl of soup and only consumed half of it. The rest went down the sink. My stomach felt heavy, as if my insides were turning to lead. Depression was a fly butting against a window pane; it buzzed and twitched at the edges of my day.

I tried to watch a film but couldn't maintain any interest. None of my books seemed interesting. Even music failed me. Everything sounded false, a poor replica of real emotions.

The man was at his window again when I went upstairs. Sitting at my desk, I watched him at his work, more brazenly this time, not caring if he saw me. I sipped at a glass of whisky, barely reading the emails I was opening on my laptop screen. Most of them were junk anyway: penis enlargement plans, payday loans, messages from fictional Nigerian bankers with money to launder. In the end I just gave up and watched the man, my whole attention focused on his presence.

It took him about an hour, but the man finally looked up from his work. He took off his glasses, wiped his mouth with the back of his hand, and stood. Leaning forward, he peered across the street, looking right at me. Smiling shyly, he made a little twitching motion with his head, and then beckoned with one hand. He was inviting me over.

"Me?" I said out loud, feeling foolish as I tapped my chest with my fingertips. "You want me to come and see you?"

As if he could hear me, the man nodded.

I think it was partly because I had nothing else to do, and partly because Kath had pissed me off by staying out with her friends, effectively underlining how little time we now had for each other. Maybe the reason doesn't even matter, just the fact that I went over there.

It was cold outside. I'd left my coat indoors but didn't want to turn back and fetch it. So I hurried across the road, walked along the path, and knocked on the man's door. When nobody answered, I knocked again. The door slowly opened.

"Hello."

He was shorter than me by about two inches, wearing a black T shirt, black jeans, and, as far as I could tell, black trainers. He opened the door further, backing away to allow me inside. Behind him, the house was dim. "Hi," he said. "Please, come in." Light glinted off the lenses of his spectacles. His skin was pale, his eyes bright and alert, and there was a couple of days' worth of dark stubble on his cheeks.

"I'm sorry... I don't even know what I'm doing here. I didn't mean to disturb you."

"It's fine," he said. "I don't get much company. Would you care for a drink?"

Once I was inside he slid behind me and shut the door, then he moved in front of me again and began to walk deeper into the house. "This way. The living room."

I followed him, looking at the monochrome and

sepia-tinted framed photos on the hallway walls: family shots taken against a backdrop of industrial landscapes; dark skies behind empty factories and tower blocks. Inside, the house was the same layout as mine. He was already pouring the drinks as I entered the main room. There was a plain beige carpet on the floor, woodchip paper on the walls, an electric fire that didn't look as if it had ever been used. The furniture was nondescript. More of those rather bleak photographs hung on the walls. There were different people in each one. For some reason I decided that none of the families in the shots were his. He'd gathered together these photos. They comprised a strange collection.

"I hope whisky's okay?" He held up a glass, rolling it between his fingers. The amber liquid held inside it glistened.

"Thanks." I took the glass. We sipped our drinks for a while, enjoying the silence.

"So," he said, breaking it with his low, quick voice. "I've seen you across there, looking through your window."

"Yes... I'm sorry. I hope you didn't think I was spying on you. It's just that, well, our windows look onto each other." I smiled but it didn't feel right, so I dropped the expression.

The man shook his head. "No, I didn't think that. Not at all. But you're probably curious about what I do up there every night." He raised his eyebrows.

"A little," I said.

"I'm a writer."

My heart sank. He was going to bore me to death about his work. "Oh. I thought you might be."

The man nodded again.

"Have you been published?" I didn't really want to know; I only asked out of politeness.

"Yes, I have, but mainly by the independent press, in limited edition printed books. I'm what they call a 'cult writer'." He almost spat those last two words out, as if they tasted of shit. His smile was brief and faded.

"I see."

We drank again. My glass was almost empty.

"Refill?" He didn't wait for me to respond, just poured me another. It was nice though, so I didn't complain.

"Are you a novelist?"

"Sometimes." He walked across to the sofa and sat down; indicated that I should do the same. "But short stories are mostly what I write." He rubbed his forehead with a small pale hand. "That's the form I'm most interested in, you see. It's the best vehicle for what I have to say."

I sat down in the armchair opposite. "Short stories, eh?"

"Mostly."

It was only then that I noticed the scratches on his arms. They were light, faded, old scars rather than fresh wounds, but I could see them through the coarse hair on his forearms. I'm still not sure why, but the sight of them filled me with a sense of dread. It was subtle, but it was there.

"Would I have heard of you?"

"Probably not." He licked his lips and took another sip of whisky. "I write under a lot of different names."

"Short stories…" I was running out of things to say.

What the hell was I doing there, anyway? I wondered if Kath might be home yet or perhaps on her way in a taxi. She would be confused if I wasn't there when she arrived home.

"Listen," I said. "I have to go. My wife... she'll be wondering where I am."

The man didn't move. He just sat there, looking at me. He wasn't threatening; he actually seemed rather sad and fragile, yet beneath it all I could detect a strength of character. "Would you like to know what my stories are about?"

"I'm sorry. I really do have to go... my wife, you see..." But I didn't stand. I couldn't. Something was holding me back. I had the feeling that he was about to tell me something of great importance; provide a revelation that would change my life forever.

"I write about tragedy. Loss. Grief. Pain. All the tragedy in the universe. I write about human suffering to try and keep it on the page and stop it from getting loose in the world." His voice was modulated, but I could tell from his eyes that he was getting excited. "If I ever stop writing, it'll be free to roam, and everything will come to an end. The days will get shorter; the nights will get darker and darker until that's all there is, one eternal night." His tone was matter-of-fact. He didn't sound at all like a maniac, despite the madness of his words.

"That's... well, that's nice." I stood and walked backwards towards the door. "Thanks for the drink."

He smiled. "I'm sorry. I didn't mean to rant like that. It's just... well, my work is very important to me. It's what keeps me going. I spend so much time up there on my own, writing, that it begins to seem like nothing else matters." He stood, setting down his glass on a cluttered little table by the chair.

I couldn't resist one final parting comment: "Okay, but what about all the tragedy that's out there. The murdered children, the abused babies, the wars, the famines, the human evil… you haven't done a very good job keeping that at bay."

He paused for a moment before speaking, not moving an inch. Then his words broke the spell. "If that level of tragedy is already out there in the world, just think of the stuff that I actually manage to hold back. Can you even imagine what that might be like? What it would do to us all?"

I couldn't… didn't want to.

"I really do have to go."

"Come back any time. You can read them if you like. My stories. I don't mind. Once they're set down on the page, they can't hurt you." He drank his whisky and flashed his spectacles at me. "Once they're written, I have power over them."

"Goodbye," I said, and turned, headed quickly for the front door. Once I was back out on the street, I glanced back at the main window. I could see him sitting there, in the same place, smiling; but when I looked upstairs, at the window opposite mine, I could see him up there too, sitting at his computer and typing his stories.

The whole thing was starting to feel like some kind of wind-up. There was a mischievous element to the man that made me think he was stringing me along with his nonsense about writing to hold back more tragedy. It sounded like a story someone like him would write. Perhaps it was even some weird kind of research.

I crossed the street and let myself back into the house. I was getting cold. I made myself a coffee and sat quietly at the kitchen table, cradling the cup between my hands, like I'd seen people do in adverts.

Kath didn't get home until very late. About 3AM. By that time, I was in bed. I pretended to be asleep as she stumbled into the room, giggling softly. She fell over when she took off her shoes, then again when she took off her clothes. She slid into bed naked, and was snoring within minutes of her head hitting the pillow.

Once I was sure she was under, I got up and went to my study, leaving off the light. He was still there, across the way, sitting in his window and writing his stories. He wasn't wearing a shirt, just a white wife-beater vest over his slim torso. This time I watched him longer than ever before: I sat there in the dark and watched him all night. Once an hour he'd stop what he was doing and scratch at his arms with his fingernails, as if digging in deep. He didn't seem to be in any pain when he did this, but nor did he seem to enjoy it. He just did it; over and over again. From where I was sitting, I was unable to see what kind of damage he was doing to his arms, but I remembered those scratches I'd seen earlier.

It seemed to me that there was some kind of correlation between what he was writing and the minor injuries he was causing himself. I didn't want to think too hard about what that might be, so I tried to ignore his violent actions, focusing only on the act of writing. His hands moved so gracefully when he typed.

I woke up at my desk without even realising I'd been asleep, feeling as if someone had just left the room. The sun was up, but it didn't seem to brighten the day. The man was no longer at his spot in the window. I looked around, at the books on my shelves, the filing cabinet, the old sporting trophies in the glass-fronted cabinet, and wondered if they were really mine. I didn't feel as if I owned anything in my life. It was all borrowed from someone else. This feeling had haunted me for years but I'd never known how to deal with it.

I went into the bedroom and stared at the unmade bed. Kath's clothes from last night were scattered upon the floor like the evidence of a sex crime. One of her shoes was by the window, the other one was under the dressing table. I could tell from the sense of absence that she was long gone. I wasn't sure if I even cared.

~

The next three days I spent away from home, working out of the Birmingham office. There was a big project going on and they needed the additional manpower. We worked ten-hour shifts, went out for a few beers afterwards, and then slept for a few hours before doing it all again. I was so busy that I forgot about my potentially crazy neighbour.

On the last night I found myself outside a pub in an area I didn't know.

Somehow I'd got split up from my workmates, or perhaps they'd deliberately dumped me. I was leaning against the wall with a lit cigarette in my hand and no idea of how I'd come to be there. I didn't even smoke, not any more. I'd given up – on Kath's insistence – a couple of years before, when we were trying for a baby that never arrived.

"Got a light?"

I glanced to my right. A young woman dressed in a skin-tight black top, a short purple dress, and knee-high boots was smiling at me.

"Well?" Her Brummie accent was strong. She had blue highlights in her long straight hair. There was a silver stud in her nose and some kind of tribal tattoo on the side of her neck. Her eyes were ringed with smeared dark makeup, as if they were bruised, or she'd been crying.

"Sorry... here." I passed her my cigarette and she used it to light the one in her hand. She sucked deeply from the cigarette, closed her eyes for a moment, and then handed mine back. I took one more drag and then stubbed it out against the wall.

"You're not from round here. I can tell by the accent."

"No. I'm from up north. Been working here."

"Ah. Right. My name's Cindy." She blew out smoke and it formed an aura around her head, obscuring her pretty face. "Wanna buy me a drink?"

"I'm married."

"So am I. Wanna buy me a drink?"

She shifted her weight from one foot to the other. Her cigarette was smoked right down to the filter, but she took one final drag before flicking it away. She smiled. Her teeth were small and very white. Her lips were thin.

"Why not."

We went back into the pub, and that was when I realised I'd never been inside before. I must have stopped for a smoke as I was passing. Christ knows who gave me the cigarette. I checked my pockets but there was no packet. At least I still had my wallet and my hotel room key, even though I had no idea where the hotel was. I couldn't even remember what it was called. I suspected my drink had been spiked. I hoped I wouldn't pass out in this strange area, with nobody to help me. I didn't want to die here, on these unforgiving streets. I had unfinished business with Kath.

The jukebox music was too loud, causing the speakers to crackle. The pub was busy but not too crowded. We managed to get a table in the corner. I went to the bar and bought us both a double Jack Daniels and coke – she was drinking it, so I'd simply followed suit.

"So," I said when I got back to the table. "What do you do?"

"What do you mean?" She was slowly nodding her head to the music; some kind of punk dirge I didn't care for.

"Like, for a job. Do you work?"

"Ah," she said. "This and that." She took a swallow of her drink. "On Tuesday and Saturday nights I strip for old married men in joints like this one. I go to Uni part time, studying psychology. I write a blog. I do shifts behind the bar in a shitty working men's club in Digbeth." She paused, smiled. "This and that."

We talked for a little while longer, but I failed to register what was being said by either of us. The music was too loud. I was too drunk. The next thing I knew we were kissing. She had her tongue in my mouth and I was sucking at it hungrily. Without speaking, she stood and took my hand, leading me outside. We walked along a narrow pathway behind the pub, then down a set of decaying concrete steps that led to a canal towpath. The black waters glistened like oil. The sky above was almost starless, stretching away into a bleak infinity. It was pitch black but somehow I could see every detail: Cindy's white skin, the tail of her tribal tattoo, the tiny scars at one corner of her mouth.

She led me to a small concrete shelter and took me inside. It was like a bus stop, but without any windows. I sat down on the hard concrete bench and she straddled me, reaching down to unzip my trousers as she kissed my face, my neck. She smelled sickly sweet; her breath was saturated in bourbon and coke. I'd never been so hard in my life. Cindy wasn't wearing any underwear. She reached down and guided me inside her and we sat there, my arse going cold on the seat, her arse in my lap. She rocked gently back and forth, and then began to move more violently, eventually slamming her backside against my cock and balls. I kept slipping out and then back in again. It hurt, but it was a good pain. I came in less than a minute, but she kept on going. She failed to achieve an orgasm, but for some reason it didn't seem to bother her.

Cindy stood and adjusted her clothing, pulling her skirt down over her shaved crotch. I pulled up my trousers, feeling cold and alone. She smiled, laughed.

"Not bad," she said.

I had no comment.

She walked to the edge of the canal, looked down at the water. She held her arms tight against her sides, had her knees pressed together. Then, as if in a dream, she stepped out onto the water but did not break the surface. As I watched, she walked out into the middle of the canal. Beneath her booted feet, the water seemed to have the flexible solidity of rubber. I could see it distorting slightly under her weight, but she did not fall through. She kept going until she reached the other side and stepped up onto the opposite bank. When she turned around, she was grinning. "I've never been able to do that before," she whispered, yet I could hear her as if she were shouting.

My head was aching as if I'd been punched in the temple. I felt sick. Trying to stand, I was aware of the earth shifting, tilting, and I threw up down the front of my shirt. Glancing up, I saw Cindy waving to me from the opposite bank. She seemed farther away now, as if the entire bank were moving, retreating from me. A small figure stood behind her. Recognition trembled through me. The figure reached up a hand and rubbed its forehead.

"Don't go," I said, but I had no idea why.

Cindy's face held an expression of sadness. Her small white hand continued to wave, and then she was swallowed up by darkness as she followed the figure away from the canal's edge and into the trees.

I fell to my knees. There were no stars in the sky because they were all in my eyes. I saw exploding novas; the universe shrunk and expanded all at once, sucking me in and then throwing me out.

When I woke up on the bench in the shelter it was early morning. Frost had formed an albino skin over the landscape. I walked back along the canal looking for the steps that would lead me back up to the pub from the night before, but I either missed them entirely or was moving in the opposite direction. Eventually I saw buildings up ahead and off to the right. I scaled the earthen bank, cut through some trees and bushes, and emerged at the side of a main road. It didn't take long to flag down a taxi, and I showed him the name of my hotel on the key fob.

"You're a long way from home, mate," he said, pulling out into the light morning traffic.

"I know," I whispered, shivering and wondering if last night had really happened or if it had all been a drunken erotic dream.

~

When I got back home I found a note from Kath. It was propped up against the salt cellar on the dining table, written in her usual messy handwritten script. The note said that she'd left me, but she wasn't sure if it was for good or just a temporary measure. She was staying at a friend's place and would contact me in a few days, once she'd made up her mind.

It was late afternoon. The sun was shuffling down behind the distant tower blocks. I sat and watched the television news for a while, trying to distract myself.

There never seemed to be any good news to report. It was all about death and destruction, job losses and factory closures. I thought about the man across the street and got up out of my chair, moving over to the window. I opened a couple of slats on the blinds and peered out. There were no lights on in his house.

Unable to settle, I left the room. At the bottom of the stairs, just as I was about to climb up to my study, I spotted something on the floor beside the front door. An A4-sized manila envelope. When I picked up the envelope, I noted that there was nothing written or printed on it. Just a blank.

Returning to the living room, I sat down and opened the envelope. Inside was a sheet of typing paper. The title at the top of the page read "Canal Dream".

I started to read.

They walked along a narrow pathway behind the pub, then down a set of decaying concrete steps that led to a canal towpath. The black waters glistened like oil. The sky above was almost starless, stretching away into a bleak infinity. It was pitch black but somehow he could see every detail: Cindy's white skin, the tail of her tribal tattoo, the tiny scars at one corner of her mouth.

She led him to a small concrete shelter and took him inside. It was like a bus stop, but without any windows. He sat down on the hard concrete bench and she straddled him, reaching down to unzip his trousers as she kissed his face, his neck. She smelled sickly sweet; her breath was saturated in bourbon and coke. He'd never been so hard in his life. Cindy wasn't wearing any underwear. She reached down and guided him inside her and they sat there, his arse going cold on the seat, her arse in his lap. She rocked gently back and forth, and then began to move more violently, eventually slamming her backside against his cock and balls. He kept slipping out and then back in again. It hurt, but it was a good pain.

He came in less than a minute, but she kept on going. She failed to achieve an orgasm, but for some reason it didn't seem to bother her.

Cindy stood and adjusted her clothing, pulling her skirt down over her shaved crotch. He pulled up his trousers, feeling cold and alone. She smiled, laughed.

"Not bad," she said.

He had no comment.

She walked to the edge of the canal, looked down at the water. She held her arms tight against her sides, had her knees pressed together. Then, as if in a dream, she stepped out onto the water but did not break the surface. As he watched, she walked out into the middle of the canal. Beneath her booted feet, the water seemed to have the solidity of rubber. He could see it distorting slightly under her weight, but she did not fall through. She kept going until she reached the other side and stepped up onto the opposite bank. When she turned around, she was grinning. "I've never been able to do that before," she whispered, yet he could hear her as if she were shouting.

His head was aching as if he'd been punched in the temple. He felt sick. Trying to stand, he was aware of the earth shifting, tilting, and he threw up down the front of his shirt. Glancing up, he saw Cindy waving to him from the opposite bank. She seemed farther away now, as if the entire bank were moving, retreating from him.

"Don't go," he said, but he had no idea why.

Cindy's face held an expression of sadness. "Come to me," she said.

He walked out into the middle of the canal, amazed at

how it supported his weight. It still looked like water, but it was solid; a pathway to epiphany.

Cindy beckoned to him from the other side of the canal. "Come on. You can make it across."

He continued walking, his skin numb and his mind travelling ahead of him. Before long he stepped onto the opposite bank, slipping briefly as he hit the incline. She reached out a hand and he took it. Her other hand was behind her back. He slipped again. She leaned towards him, gripping him tighter and tighter. Her other hand appeared from behind her back. Something glinted in her fist, catching the moonlight. It flashed through the air towards him. Because of his position a little way down the bank, he was looking up, his throat exposed. The sharp edge of the knife blade cut him clean across the Adam's apple, neatly bisecting it. He choked on bloody words that devolved into crooks. Falling to his knees, he looked up into her eyes. She was smiling.

He fell face down on the hard-packed earth and bled out into the night.

Cindy retreated into darkness, licking the blood from her fingers. She was nothing, not even a dream, or the rumour of a dream. Before long, it was as if she had never even existed.

I crumpled the sheet of paper in my fist but hung onto it, not wanting to let it go. My memory latched onto the image of that small figure on the canal bank, standing behind the woman who'd called herself Cindy. What was he doing there? Had he rewritten my own tragedy in order to save me, or to prove to me that he'd been telling the truth all along? Or had I imagined the whole thing? Was I hallucinating even now? At the time, I'd thought my drink had been spiked, but now

I was certain. The way I'd come to outside that pub, the way I had followed the woman without even questioning her motives, the strange vision of her walking across the canal water, the figure in the shadows behind her. None of it could have been real.

I went to the front door and opened it. There was now a light on across the road. The man's upstairs room was occupied. Shutting the door, I stepped outside and went across the street. I walked up to his door and rang the bell. Keeping my finger on the buzzer, l tried to remain calm.

The door opened. He was standing there on the threshold in the same black T-shirt, black trousers and black trainers he'd been wearing the first time we spoke. He was even wearing the same glasses. He rubbed his forehead, pushing back the hair to show me part of his scalp.

I wasted no time. "Who are you?"

"Call me Erik. With a K, I always liked that name."

"No, not your name... who are you?"

"I'm nobody, just a writer. I'm someone who writes stories."

"How did you know...how do you know what happened? Were you there? Or did you put the images inside my head?"

"I don't know what you mean. Please, you seem agitated. Why don't you come in?"

I followed him inside. This time he started climbing

the stairs. "Up here. In my writing room. It's the cosiest part of the house. I have all the other radiators switched off because I only ever spend time up here."

Watching Erik's narrow, black-clad back, I climbed the stairs behind him. The lights were off apart from the one in his writing room: I could see the glow spilling across the landing and down the first few steps.

"This way," he said, entering the lighted room.

The walls of the small room were decorated with yet more photos of industrial landscapes, some with people in the foreground and some without. Several of them featured what looked like corpses under sheets or wrapped up in body bags. I suspected they were crime scene photos.

"Look at this," said Erik, rummaging in a drawer on his writing desk – a compact piece of mass-produced flat-pack furniture that was pushed up against the wall under the single window. He pressed a newspaper into my hands. It was a local paper, printed in Birmingham. The front page headline was about a series of murders; over the past six months the bodies of several men had been found with their throats cut down by some canal behind an old pub.

I looked up from the printed page and into his face. Behind the glasses, his eyes sparkled. "Do you see?"

Shaking my head, I dropped the newspaper onto the floor. The pages spread apart like skeins of slashed, bloodless flesh. My feet shuffled on the cheap carpet as I backed away, coming up against the opposite wall. I pressed the palms of my hands against the woodchip wallpaper. In the room's harsh light, I could make out more of those scratches on Erik's bare arms. Some of them had scabbed over; he must have drawn blood.

"What's happening here? What are you doing?"

He shook his head. "I'm a writer. I told you that. I write. That's all I do. I write it all down in the hope that it won't happen, and sometimes —just sometimes – it works." He gestured at the shelves on the walls. They were filled with black box-files.

"All this... all my work. It's my life's work." He looked desperate, forlorn; he was reaching out, trying to make a connection, but he lacked the emotional tools to do it properly.

How long had he been doing this, and why? Who had set him out on this thankless task, this endless project? I imagined him sitting here for years, typing, scratching at his arms, his legs, other parts of his body I was unable to see. Pouring all of his justified rage at the world into these writings, imagining that he was making some kind of difference by noting it all down, transcribing the terrors he thought would happen if he didn't get them down onto the page.

It was pathetic. He was pathetic. A sad, pathetic little man... or was he? Had my experience last night shown me nothing? Was I going to ignore what had happened to me, mark it down as the result of a spiked drink and a raging libido? If that newspaper report was correct, then the only conclusion here – logical or otherwise – was that Erik had saved my life. He'd written a new ending to my late-night encounter, cannibalising my potential tragedy for one of his tales so that I might survive.

He moved towards me, not quickly, just at normal

speed. I'm not sure why I reacted the way I did, but my hand made a fist and shot out, connecting with the side of his head as he approached me. He went down onto one knee, raised a hand to the point of impact, and blinked at me through the shiny lenses of his specs.

"I'm…I'm sorry," I said.

"It's okay. This must be confusing for you. It took me decades to understand what it was all about, and I'm still not even sure. I can appreciate your anger."

His lack of aggression made me feel more aggrieved. I stormed out of the room, down the stairs, and marched across the road. As I shut my front door, locking out the night and whatever madness it held, I glanced up at Erik's writing room window. He was already sitting in his chair, typing, as if none of this had happened. Just as I knew he would be.

~

The following day I called Kath on the phone. To my surprise, she answered straight away.

"Hello." Her voice was detached. There was a coldness there I'd not experienced before.

"We need to talk."

She laughed bitterly. "Jesus, were you always so clichéd?"

"Probably. Now, when are we going to fucking talk?"

"That's more like it. At last there's some fire in your belly."

I didn't respond.

"I don't want to talk, not to you. The time for talking is long gone. I've made a decision, and it's that I never want to see you again. I don't even want to come round for my stuff. I'll send someone with a van. They can collect it for me."

I stared at the wall, wishing that I could kick it down but knowing I was too weak to even try. "What did I ever do?"

"It's what you didn't do. You didn't love me enough. You didn't give me a baby. You never, ever understood me. You didn't even try."

The line went dead. She was gone; gone forever. Somehow I'd imagined it being less abrupt.

~

I spent the rest of the weekend in a daze, drinking vodka, looking through old photographs of what I thought were happier times but were really just the calm before the emotional storm. She was not smiling in any of them. Oh, there was the occasional half-smile, or an expression that seemed more than half way there, but nothing you could ever describe as natural.

I'd never made her happy. That truth, more than any other, was tough to face. Thinking about it then, I realised that she'd never given me happiness either, not really. All we'd ever done was pretend. Our entire relationship was based on an idea of what couples were meant to do, what they were supposed to feel, rather than anything we'd actually felt for each other.

Whenever I tried to sleep, my head was filled with images of that Birmingham canal, the girl walking out across the water, the small figure on the other side. The girl, Cindy, became Kath; the figure in the shadows was me, then it was Erik, and finally it was someone I'd never seen before. The stories were becoming confused, their plotlines knotting together to form a sticking point. The only common feature was Erik. He was the author of something much larger than himself.

By Sunday night I was sick and tired of drinking. The living room floor was littered with empty takeaway boxes. My clothes smelled of kebab meat and chilli sauce. My mouth tasted like it belonged to someone else, a person who liked to lick under the rim of toilet bowls.

I didn't know what to do so I ordered another takeaway. By the time the pizza arrived, I'd lost my appetite, so I threw it in the bin and drank the large bottle of no-name cola that came with it. I went up to my study, thinking that I might log onto the internet and watch some porn. Then I looked across the street and saw Erik sitting in his writing room window.

Things had changed since I'd last seen him.

He was naked – at least from the waist up. He looked thinner than before, almost to the point of emaciation. His pale, skinny arms were furred from countless new scratches. At that distance, I couldn't make out if there was any blood. His glasses hung at an angle on his narrow face. Even from my study I could see that his cheeks were shredded; the skin hung in thin, bloodless strips, like pages partially pulled from the spine of a book. Despite all of this, and his obvious discomfort, he kept on typing.

I left the house and walked across the street. It felt like it might be the last time. I knocked on his door but there was no answer. When I tried the door it was locked. Walking around the side of the house, I spotted an open kitchen window. He was in trouble. I had to help if I could. Never mind what he'd done, or what I thought he'd done, this was a situation I couldn't ignore.

I grabbed a nearby wheely bin, moved it across to beneath the window, and used it to climb up onto the window sill. The window was small, but I managed to lean through and unlatch the larger window from the inside and use that to gain access.

Once inside the house, I headed straight up to his room. There was a candle burning on the floor. The single light bulb hanging from the ceiling above his head had shattered; there were diamonds of glass on the floor around his chair. The glass in the picture frames on his wall had been broken. Some of it was bloody, as if he'd gone round punching them all.

"Hello..." I still didn't know what I was going to do. "Erik... are you okay?"

I could see now that he was in fact completely naked, but his legs were bent into an odd shape, the joints buckled out of true. They looked broken. He sat there like a man in a trance, just typing. His short but elegant fingers were the only part of his body that had not been mutilated. Every other inch of him sported some kind of wound: a scratch, a cut, a livid welt.

All the tragedy in the universe... His words from our first meeting echoed inside my head, and then in the room. He'd been trying to make a connection, to tell me something important, and I'd ignored him. I wondered how many other people had done the same until finally it had all become too much for him and had led to this point in time.

Slowly, I approached him from behind, reaching out to grab his gashed shoulder. The torn skin beneath my fingers felt warm, spongy, but there was no blood. "Please stop."

He kept on typing.

I spun his chair around one-hundred-and-eighty degrees so that he was facing me. His fingers were still moving, as if he were still typing at the keyboard. Behind him, the keys continued to make a harsh clicking sound, as if his fingers still worked them.

...just think of the stuff that I actually manage to hold back. Can you even imagine what that might be like?

"Please..."

His face was a mess. At the corners of his mouth the cheeks were sliced clean through, like a Chelsea Smile: I could see his yellowed teeth through the slits. His glasses were broken, the lenses shattered. But it didn't matter because his eyes had been pushed deep into their sockets – perhaps by him, or perhaps by someone else, I couldn't be certain. His nose was flattened, as if from a heavy blow. His hair had almost totally fallen out, and he had two cauliflower ears, like those of a retired pugilist.

Despite everything, his hands still moved at the ends of his floppy wrists, the fingers typing steadily away at ghost keys.

"I don't understand."

He didn't answer me. He couldn't hear. Wherever he was now it was cold and dark and silent, and there were more stories to tell. There were no stars, no moon, no hours of daylight. It was all one long, dark night, and he was lost within its silken folds. My rejection had sent him scampering into a fictional realm, a place where all the landscapes were bleak and industrial and everyone was a stranger. I wondered if Cindy, the killer he'd written out of my plot, was there waiting for him, knife in hand, thin lips parted and ready to taste his blood...

I grabbed him again by the shoulders, trying not to think about how much they felt like raw meat, and lightly shook him. His toothless mouth dropped open; inside, darkness twitched and crawled up from the back of his throat like a thick black worm.

I felt tears on my cheeks. "Tell me how it ends," I whispered, choking back sobs. "Tell me how the story ends."

Erik's fingers finally stopped typing. Behind him, at the window, another kind of darkness – this one greater, blacker, and hungry – swept in from a distant place, covering the cars, the street, the houses. And that was when the truth finally hit me; that his stories truly mattered, had always mattered. Perhaps they were the only ones that ever would.

~

In English myth there exists the notion of the Sin-eater. The term refers to a person who, through the means of ritual, took on the sins of a household. They would be passed bread and ale over the dying body of a person, and by consuming these things they absorbed the dying person's sins and cleansed them for their passage into the afterlife.

This is called apotropaic magic; a type of magic intended to turn away harm. In modern times, might that role have mutated into something else? In an age of rampant commercialism and psychotic consumerism – times when all art is deemed useless, lacking real value – might not an artist adopt the role of a sin-eater for the whole of society? And if we are to accept this theory, who is to say that the job might not be entrusted to just one person, an obscure writer of dark fiction?

It is now six months since the unexplained death of the man I knew as Erik. Things have got worse, or so it seems. The nights are darker than they used to be. The days are no longer bright. I try to tell myself that it's coincidental, and the world was heading this way all along. Sometimes I even pretend to believe it.

Last night, when I turned on the evening news, there was a report about the recent mass shootings in Birmingham, Manchester, Leeds and Newcastle: fifty-seven dead, another twenty still in critical condition. This was followed by an item about the East London rape gangs. Things like this never used to happen, not of such magnitude. Tragedy has accelerated; we as a society are nearing some kind of critical mass. There's no empathy left, no human compassion. Scenes like those I saw on television are now a common occurrence.

After watching the news for as long as I could, I switched off the television and went to bed. The manila envelope I'd found on the hallway floor was on my bedside table. I picked it up, paused for a moment, and then opened it. I already knew what I would find inside.

This time there was no story typed on the single A4 page. Just five words in bold font; a simple statement:

This is how the story ends.

the girl with dark hair

Morning

The girl with dark hair woke suddenly and with a start as the tiny metal bell of the mechanical alarm clock tore through her nightmares. She sat bolt upright in bed, pushing the covers to the dusty hardwood floor. It was the same routine every morning. The first few seconds of her day were a time of sheer terror. The confusion of the unknown which then, as her brains cells engaged, flooded with the oxygen of her rapid breathing, sharpened back into focus.

And, the real world that greeted her was just a few degrees of improvement over the faceless phantoms of her night terrors. She swung around in bed and placed both feet on the cold floor. It was only September and yet already she felt a slight chill in the air. A portent of what was to come. She made a mental note to stock up on woollen rugs and blankets before then. Despite the future discomfort of the freezing weather ahead, she prayed to Allah for it. She prayed for the icy winter months when it would be safe for her to wander the streets of the desolate city once more.

Maybe she'd leave?

It was a sick joke of a metropolis now anyway, empty of its people, devoid of any human movement. A city without the living is no city at all. It was a sepulchral reflection of what it once was, peopled only by the dead. She was living in a concrete necropolis, a cemetery memorial to humanity, complete with deathly quiet highways and cold, sullen and empty apartment tombs. Only of course there was life in the city. It teemed with lives. The thought chilled her further so she got dressed, unbolted the bedroom door locks and left the damp windowless room which was her nocturnal shelter.

Opening the white paint-cracked wooden shutters in the kitchen, she could see that they had already started work out in the square. A long column of shiny black backs trotted down the street in near perfect military order. On the right were un-laden workers, looting some new structure which somehow met their unique requirements. On the left were creatures struggling back, carrying giant sheets of corrugated metal in their incisors. The heavily laden workers tacked left and right as they fought to control their direction whilst carrying many times their own bodyweight.

She had once admired the tireless work ethic of the ants but after months of survival in a city dominated by such creatures, she now had a clear understanding of where she fits into their ordered world. A position in between marginal threat and potential food source. By watching the last of the survivors being ripped in two, she had learned not to cross the supply route of a colony and not to venture too close to a nest. An ant attack is a grisly spectacle to behold and each hive is violently territorial. Legions of the smaller workers would nip and claw at any threat before the larger armoured soldiers stormed in, firing thin jets of acidic bile and cutting limbs like paper. When the ants were on the move, it was best to leave them to complete their schedule. But, she envied their communism. They were never alone by being part of their insectoid tribe.

The girl with dark hair pulled back the shutters completely and a weak autumn sun strayed through an overcast grey sky.

The kitchen was a large one, with chunky Shaker-style units three quarters of the way around and a rustic looking table dominating the centre. Several of the oak cupboards lacked doors and their exposed metal hinges jutted out like evacuated orphans at a railway station. Some had clearly been torn from their position in desperation, in some frantic attempt to fortify the house against intruders. Lacking any covers, it was easier for her to see the fruits of her foraging in the cupboards. The shelves were half-full, stacked with tinned cans of peaches, soups and a lonely tin of processed meat which she tried not to think about. She'd survived Halal for the first months of the crisis but she'd pushed it to the back of her mind recently. It was permitted in extremis and these were certainly such times.

A guilty conscience is oft a prompt to action and she peered over into the corner where a prayer mat lay rolled neatly. She took it and laid it in front of the window, allowing the faint sun glow to touch her pallid face. She knelt down and prayed. Something she hadn't done for at least two weeks.

"Merciful Allah, look upon me, your servant and save me from the trials of these times. I am alone and lost in the stony desert. Hear me cry in the rocky wilderness."

After a few spoken words, her prayers continued in silence, descending into a childish wish list of items from a few hard showers of rain to a pleading request to find other survivors. Such are the small demands of the lonely.

University

As our climate warms so," emphasised the dull professor, "the whole biosphere will adapt. It is not the first time and it won't be the last," he called out to the blank and sterile faces.

The heat of the afternoon overwhelmed the feeble conditioning units in each corner of the auditorium and the brain dead teenagers waned and slouched in their uncomfortable wooden lecture hall seating. The older generation lectured the younger on the ill-effects of their own creation and the youth strained to contain their obvious boredom.

"Why is he telling us this crap," whispered a student with a calculator. "It's a geriatric guilt trip," came the answer, "they know they've fucked the world but they want to make sure that we know." The large plasma screen flicked on as the dull professor switched slides to another map. By clicking on a small arrow, the image came to life, with blue merging into green and gradually becoming the dominant colour. He offered a monotone commentary of the impact on the world like some wavering priest reading from a clichéd gospel he no longer believed in.

He too, was tired like his students. He had repeated this new orthodoxy for the last five years to an endless sea of vacant faces. Two questions hid in the back of his mind. Firstly, how long before they change the orthodoxy?

Denial had been *en vogue* when he first started giving this course and a change in policy had meant hours for him updating hundreds of slides and over a thousand pages of course notes.

Secondly, who really cared anyway? He was telling miners trapped in a collapsed coal shaft that the oxygen was running out and there was little they could do about it.

It was as if some part of his generation wanted all of its sins laid bare, to be adjudicated by the younger generation. To be judged by the student with the calculator who could hardly keep his eyes open. In truth, the jurors were most disinterested in this inter-generational court. The defence was one of hollow words and the animosity of the first few years was gone. The violent student protests which the dull professor had once supported were now silent. Few under 30 cared. There was no future in the way the pre-enders understood it. That's what they called people who had already lived a full life before the changes. Pre-enders had brought us here. They'd lived well up to now. From here on it was change and a change for the worse. And it was speeding up.

The dull professor presented another slide and then another. A sequence of images showed the movement of animal and insect populations against climate change. It showed large ferocious red ants on the tip of a peninsula.

"That's a lie," whispered the student with the calculator, "my parents had to kill a nest of these fuckers last year at their cabin in the mountains."

The dull professor heard him but chose to ignore it. He was paid to deliver the lectures and what's more on an hourly basis. He wasn't paid to bolster the semi-truths he spoke.

The girl with dark hair sat at the back of the auditorium, scanning through the pages of a dog-eared illegal nature journal. These curiously academic but also banned pamphlets professed to offer another truth to generation zero.

"It is vital that the truth is told," spoke one in poorly printed black letters. **"Our objective is to educate and warn. The future for generation zero will be a battle for survival on this planet."**

She turned a few more pages. Crude and poorly edited reader's comments about giant arachnids and mutated wasps that fire their stings like some cartoon Amazonian native with an angry blow pipe. The general commotion and outbreak of shuffling indicated that the lecture had finished and she added to the noise by starting to pack up her stuff. As looked she up, the dull professor was still spouting, his voice barely audible over the banging and zipping. A couple was engaged in a passionate embrace in the corner of the room and their heaving grunts soon infected the noisescape. As the boy started to pull down his trousers, the girl with dark hair scooped up her things and left, trying not to look at the lewd girl as she fawned ecstasy. Crowds walked past the two as they engaged in their open love making. One got the impression they were not doing this as part of some sexual thrill, of doing it in sight of the world. It was just an impulse. They felt like having sex, so they did. Generation zero cared little for social norms. These barriers belonged to the pre-enders. Posters warned of more murders on campus as she walked through the shabby grey corridor towards the quadrangle. The police had all but abandoned the district. The colour image of a grisly rape posted on the wall scared her and she walked briskly off towards her rooms, sticking to the most populated foot paths.

"Where you going towel head," screamed an angry white man from the trees. "Why don't we see what you're hiding under there sweet heart?!" She daren't look at him but the angry white man continued to rant, empty cans of strong beer littering the ground around him like rotten fallen apples. Her hijab was making her a target every time she went out now. She would have to stop wearing it. "I'll do you from behind," was the last threat she heard as she rounded a corner in the quadrangle and tailed a convoy of other students. A tall African man turned to her.

"Alright sister?"

"I'm OK, thanks." She stared for an instant into his slate-grey eyes. He was wearing the bright blue head scarf of the desert people. She hadn't realised any of them were left. The angry white man visibly retreated back to his alcohol soaked nest under the leaf-less tree. "Don't you come out with that on again sister," he warned. She looked at the path, managing a nod before he turned back and headed across the parched and cracking pavement.

She reached her apartment without further incident. She'd stopped at the express shop en route and picked up ten more cans of soup. The weak blue plastic bag had almost given way on her way back but it had held. Much as the whole city was holding on. Just about. The structures and vestiges of order were there; the shadow of civilisation remained but the bones and muscle of the state had long since disintegrated. State benefits had become irregular and now stopped altogether. Police numbers dwindled as their bank paid salaries evaporated into the unsettled air. None of them risked their lives in the increasing spiral of street violence. None that wanted to live anyway.

She bolted the door shut and switched the television on, hoping to catch the afternoon news. A sarcastic newsreader taunted a bearded expert as he professed theories on species movement and mutation. The news programme flicked to a live interview with an elderly grey-haired lady protesting at the massacre of the growing wolf population in the hills before a local cut in on air.

"Easy for you to say," said the sun-tanned farmer, "they haven't just ripped your grandchildren from their cots."

There was a loud cry of agreement from the invisible spectators. The girl with dark hair filled the kettle and switched it on. A few minutes later she returned and poured the water into her cup, flooding a mint tea bag. The water turned a very faint green colour but had no strength. She tested the water. It was cold. The television now silent. The power was down, again.

Voices

She stood on the broken glass looking into the darkness of the shopping arcade. The tiny newsagent's booth on her right had been ransacked and the scorch marks around the advertising placard hinted at a violent past. She had never understood the human fascination with fire. There are many degrees of irony in man but none she thought as evident and contradictory as this. The collapse of civilisation under the insectoid onslaught had left millions of city dwellers hungry and yet time after time, she had witnessed looters burning the very shops in which edible supplies may still be found. She scooted past the designer stores. Several appeared to be completely intact as if their spray-tanned and preened shop purveyors had just closed after a busy Saturday. This time never to return. Their shops now stood like sealed museums to elegant goods from another world. Branded luxury handbags and shoes of crocodile skin and soft leather now lay useless in this hard new reality. She paused for a moment to admire the worn-look russet leather handbag in the window display. 3000 read the price tag. More irony she thought.

There was that much cash blowing around in the street outside. Worthless paper for a worthless item. Still, she made a note of the store all the same.

Her target for the second time this week was the outdoor camping store on the first floor. She had stuffed a bag full of small blue camping gas cylinders on her last visit, along with an almost full box of stale oat energy bars. It had been like eating sugary cardboard as she worked her way through them but they were nutritious and most of all they were sweet. Mankind's new rival on earth had devoured so much of the sugary food out there that this was a rare find, so she broke one of her primary rules and returned to a looting scene to harvest more supplies. She could live on a bar a day along with the few other items she'd foraged. A box held 24 bars. The maths was simple but brutal. That's 24 more days of survival. Her life had been reduced to that. She no longer thought in years as people used to before the fall. A day alive was an achievement. A day avoiding death was on its own a minor victory.

She reached the camping shop and noted the position of the metal bin and plank she'd carefully laid across the entrance. It was untouched, the empty cans she had balanced around the doorway still there. No bugs, she concluded.

She flicked on her torch and shone it into the semi-darkness of the store. The man in the hat was still there, standing like a guardian over the all-weather jacket display.

"How's business?" she asked.

"*Good, good,*" he replied.

"I'm back for some more energy bars." He nodded. "Do you think you'll be ordering anymore?"

"*Unlikely, problems with the supplier.*" She propped her

torch on one of the shelves so its protective beam of light spread across a good half of the store and bathed the areas she was targeting in dull shadows. "I'll just help myself then," she said as she breezed past the man in the hat.

"*There's no more camping gas,*" he called after her.

"That's OK," she said out loud. It was the first time she'd spoken in almost a week and the vibrations shocked her. The man in the hat stood silently as he always did. She wondered if he'd sold any of those waterproof fishing hats. She noticed one of his pale plastic hands was missing.

She reached the trekking supplies shelf and swept a hand along, scooping all of the remaining bars into a large green backpack. She picked through the contents, removing one which appeared to have been nibbled by rodents and another whose wrapper was torn. She couldn't chance infected food. The sick and injured were easy prey for them. Before the fall, people had always spoken of insects as cold and calculating but during the uprising; they had also proved remarkably adept at sensing weakness and injury.

She paused from rifling through her bag, tilting her head slightly to the right, momentarily holding her breath that she might hear more intently. She started her sorting only to stop again. It was a faint noise coming from the food court in the basement. Not a scurrying or ticking. The noises they usually make. She waited in silence, daring not make the slightest move lest she lose a tenuous link with another. Again, the noise. This time, she was sure. It was a faint cry. Faint, only due to distance. It was a male voice calling. She could not make out what was being said.

She zipped up her back pack and moved out of the shop. She didn't pay and the man in the hat didn't stop her. She leant over the glass railings and looked down towards the shadows in the food court. A coffee concession stand had been upended, sending paper cups all over the floor. The fixed plastic chairs and tables had been smashed and broken. She strained to listen in the silence. There was no sound other than the dusty breeze blowing through the empty corridors. The cry echoed again. She still could not make out what was being said. It was as if the crier was injured or drunk. She felt the beating of her heart inside as it tried to escape her ribcage. Panic seeped through her face and her left eyelid twitched like it did when she was nervous.

Light refracted through the cracked glass roof of the shopping centre, sending welcome luminescence into the dark corners. She thought she heard a scampering noise. But surveying the injured landscape she could see nothing.

"Hello," she called softly, "anyone there?" No answer.

An unbearable pause persisted, less than a few seconds but abject torture for the lonely. It was broken by a clear cry in the weak sunlight. "Help! Help me!"

Was it a statement or a question? A call for aid or a subconscious warning to stay away from one member of an endangered species to another.

Her mind flickered back a few months to her first refuge by the main square, an unapologetic glass tower overlooking the metro station. A penthouse apartment high aboveground, she chose it because it was flooded with sunlight virtually the whole day and at the time, the dark was a particular fear for her. It was also the last time she'd seen another living human, it was a kid in a green coat calling for his mother near the underground station.

~

Through the falling rain she'd heard the cries and nudged up to a tall window to watch from the safety of her lofty hideaway. The kid in the green coat was making enough noise to attract every creature within a mile; the vibrations alone would bring the arachnids crawling from their dark holes. Those rare black hunters were normally found camping in dark dry places where no sensible human would ever tread. At least not now.

The old world was one of helping strangers, of carrying shopping bags for old people and standing up for pregnant women. The new world had recast the old world's morals. She stood watching the child in the street, half-tempted to make a move. The kid in the green coat was within her reach. She could call from the window. She had enough food to spare but she remained still, glued to the spot. She finally looked away and pretended to consult some torn city map. Within minutes, the crying stopped and when she next glanced out, all that was left of the child was a violent red stain on the pavement and a ripped green coat.

"It's not my job to save the world." Her mind returned to present events.

The cries from the Food Court increased as if sensing a nearby listener, like an invisible fishing line, yanking at her. Why move now? What was so different now? The darkness of the lower floor was an alarm bell. The girl of a few months ago would have crept out and returned to her fortress. Alone but safe. Always alone but always safe.

But this was now. Months of not seeing another living person. A loneliness which reading only exacerbated by reminding her that there had once been a world, a human world of interactions, of stories and of romance.

This time she moved. She grabbed a wooden plank from a smashed bench nearby and headed down the glass staircase to the food court. She panicked briefly as a grey cloud passed over the sun, recasting the scene in an eerie darkness again but this was just an interlude and the light soon returned.

At the bottom of the stairs, she stopped and froze on the spot, listening intently for the noise.

"Help me," came the cry. Repeated again, she could triangulate its location. It was inside the bright red fast food concession. "Hello," she called, "are you injured?" The same broadcast was repeated, like a scratched record.

As she moved towards the concession, she noticed that the security shutters had been savaged and were now drenched in insectoid body parts and dried blackness.

She was spooked but determined. Determined not to be alone. Not to allow the knowledge of abandoning another human haunt her. It wasn't fair, this life. She briefly wondered if there really was a pair of cosmic scales somewhere weighing human souls in terms of good and evil deeds.

Then it emerged from the shadows.

Atonement

It tore down the metal grill as it forced its way out of the fast food concession. It was a vile, vicious-looking insect with six barbed legs spraying over the tills and cupboards in an effort to maintain a balance. Its head was a shiny black and poked through into the forecourt, followed by the rest of its body. She could see nothing of its thorax, for its broad body, measuring maybe six feet by six feet was covered in severed limbs and other human body parts which looked to have been moulded on with some kind of yellowy resin. On top of the creature, she could see a waving hand. One of the creature's macabre human decorations was alive. The legless torso wobbled from side to side in a gooey mash of putrid fudge, its bleeding stumps sealed with sap-like glue.

A long proboscis poked into the food court and after targeting its prey, jetted a stream of yellow bile. The flow of toxin missed her face by a few inches but a splash caught her ear and her flesh singed and shrivelled in the acid.

Just as the near-corpse on the creatures back howled, the creature itself opened its mandibles and emitted an inhuman scream, a tempting echo of a human cry for help. A deadly mimic.

She turned her back and dashed for the static escalator. She threw an empty bin out of the way as she charged through. The giant assassin bug emerged from its lair and fired another stream of poison. This time it landed on the plastic handrail of the escalator. The hand rail soon bubbled and hissed under the acidic attack. She clutched her ear as she ran upstairs and out of the shopping mall. A splash of the acid started to burn her hand. She grabbed her water bottle and poured it over her ear and hands. The burning slowed but putting a hand to her ear, she could feel a chunk missing, dissolved. It was red and raw, delivering a driving pain.

Alone

The girl with dark hair stared out of the window at the grey sky and drizzle. Ant debris littered the square but most of the workers were gone, leaving a solitary soldier standing guard like a glistening marble statue at the end of the street. The only sign that it was living was the occasional tilt of its head. Standing almost four feet in height and with legs spanning six feet, the soldier ant was an impressive creature, vigilant, unquestioning and wholly capable of remorseless violence. It was the perfect soldier. Incapable of mercy, devoid of morals and inextricably bound to the survival of the hive. Without the hive the soldier would die. Without the soldier the hive would soon be ravaged and die. A perfect symbiotic relationship she thought. Not an equal relationship of course, for the solider-ant could be ordered to sacrifice itself at any time. She envied its purpose and its community. The creature stood in the cold rain, dormant and alone but in truth, it was not alone. It was a component of an extended network of family. Something she had not known for many months.

After the escape at the shopping centre, the girl with dark hair was too nervous to leave the block. Every time she closed her eyes, nightmare images of the assassin bug flooded her mind, the dismembered bodies snagged to it by vile yellow mucus. The hellish echo as it feigned speech to lure in its prey. The pathetic moan of those half-corpses still alive and, in particular, the man without legs, his stumps cauterized by the burning acid of the creature's primary weapon.

She plunged her face into the bowl of rainwater she'd been keeping for washing. It felt good as she rubbed her hands deep into her face, to clean off the grime of the abandoned streets, to scrub off the murderous residue of the assassin bug; whose macabre travelling mortuary, she had almost been added to.

The cold water refreshed her and after drying, she unbolted the apartment door and peeked into the corridor. All was quiet and still, exactly as it should be. The front door was still blocked, as far as she knew. The three foot planks of wood still hammered and nailed across it. The sweet stench of decay still permeated through the gaps. She crept up a floor and went to the front window of the dusty and faded hallway. She carefully leveraged the opening and pushed her head into the morning air. Immediately, she heard the deep, humming buzz of the blue bottles as they hovered low after a night of feeding. Looking down, she could see one of the creatures, poking its long proboscis through the masonry of the wall of the basement flat and into the apartment.

It must have found something in the flat below.

Beside it were the dried and split open remains of a body. A neighbour perhaps, but she could not be sure as so little of the corpse remained. It was a shell of something human. At the bottom of the stairs lay a bloated bubble of a body, the chest cavity of which seemed to rise and fall like it was populated by an over-sized beating heart. The busy blue bottles, most the size of a man's head, were carrion and would trawl the city for the suitable dead. Anything they found would be dragged back to the nest, such as they had made on the front stairs to the apartment block. The blue bottles would then graft their thousands of tiny white eggs just under the epidermis of the skin. A scene from Hades she knew was just outside her door. She toyed with the idea of burning them all. Of killing the ghoulish flies. But, the stench seemed to keep the ants away. She didn't know how but why risk it?

Her attention was caught by movement in the corner of her eye. Just by the front door, she watched a giant blue bottle struggling with a flabby white corpse. She studied it closely as the creature stabbed its sickly white eggs into the thick fleshy thigh of the body. Suddenly, the eyes of the body flickered open, its arms spread out as if simulating a crucifixion. It stared up, seeking mercy from the heavens but no deity responded. Mercy for mankind, it seemed, had been exhausted. Patience replaced by alienation.

She could not look away as the fat woman mocked a scream and lifted a weak arm from the pavement. Did she really expect help?

Blue bottles feed on the dead but it wasn't the first time she'd seen them insert their eggs into the half-living. In a few days, the larvae would emerge and feast their way through the dying woman. She quietly pulled her head back inside and closed the window. The fat woman would be dead soon, she hoped. Or else too weak to scream, as the ravenous young of the blue bottle nipped and gorged through her leg muscle and up into her podgy stomach cavity. If she'd had a gun, she would have shot the fat woman from the window. At least sparing her the last hours of excruciating pain. She toyed with the idea of dropping something on her, maybe of smashing the head but the thought quickly evaporated as the closed window muffled the funeral buzz of the flies outside.

Hope dies slowly when you are alone and, as she rifled through the other apartments in the block, she felt it more keenly than ever. She'd visited them before of course, in the early days, when she was fussier about what she would and would not eat. She had left the tinned ham on the shelves, cans of mushy peas, tinned pineapple she hated. They were her reserve. Scattered around the block and with her supplies dwindling she was forced to gather them. During this second trawl, she looked with hungry eyes, eyes which are coloured by the threat of starvation. And an empty stomach focuses the mind.

This time she gathered all of the cans, even the processed ham. She knew it was something she should have done earlier but she still hesitated to enter the apartments of people she once knew, her neighbours. Stepping inside one apartment was like treading on the grave of a friend and as she entered, the temperature and hint of damp immediately told her that these rooms were exposed to the elements.

Sure enough, she found a window smashed and patches of dried liquid strewn around the cupboards and fridge. The blue bottles had found a way in. Looking over the grey slate worktops in the kitchen, she noticed a clutch of white eggs the size of golf balls nestled in the corner, in an area where the blue tiles had been pulled away. They were translucent and she could see they were three quarters full of liquid. Each contained a floating black maggot-looking body, about half the size of her little finger.

For a few seconds she considered it. She could collect up the eggs. Maybe the watery pus inside was nutritious and full of vitamins. Maybe the giant blue bottle eggs were a delicacy in another part of the world. She doubted it and the slight wrench in her stomach told her that she was not quite that hungry. Her appetite was not aided by the crudely torn human body parts which festered and rotted around the egg sacks. The dead flesh was to be a feast for the ravenous larvae when they emerged.

The carefully framed photographs scattered around the walls of the apartment made her uncomfortable. Their still faces judged her intrusion and she quickly scouted the other rooms, gathering up a new tube of toothpaste from the bathroom before leaving.

It was almost mid-day by the time her search was completed and she returned to her apartment and locked the doors once more. She hadn't eaten so far and yet she felt no hunger. Her body was starving but she felt no compunction to fill it with fuel. Her military fatigues hung loosely around her skeletal waist and a lack of energy prevented her from completing any of the projects she lined up to prevent her stagnating in isolation.

She curled up on the sofa, pulling a blanket over her legs and started to re-read Pride and Prejudice. The complex sentences and obscure words danced in front of her eyes and she struggled to concentrate. A book demands something of its reader. It is not as passive as, for example, the television or the cinema, where the viewer is fed a steady diet of sound and moving picture.

She had always loved books and had tried her own hand at creative writing. Now, even with endless quiet hours, the classics lay unread and her notebooks empty. It was not like her mind was pregnant with ideas. She was a blank. Her imagination had disappeared along with the rest of humanity. To escape into a book one must feel safe enough to leave the corporeal and material world behind. A book can be both an escape and a refuge. She did not feel safe and so none of Austen's acute observations pierced the hard shell of realism around her.

She put the book down and closed her eyes. What's the point, whispered her conscience as she sought sleep. What is there left to hope for? She could not answer so brushed such thoughts aside in favour of oblivion, if only for a few hours.

Life happens between dawn and dusk. There is little outside these solar markers unless you have either a lover or are a dreamer of dreams. This is the ruse Allah has played on man such that his seventy years are cut by half as he lays in unconscious slumber. And, the girl with dark hair had neither a lover nor dreams. She slept alone and her nights were passionless and lonely. Her mind was dull and dreamless. She had no hopes for the future and it is on this fruitful soil that dreams are made.

She slipped instead into a vacuous sleep and did not rouse again until dawn.

Radio

Such is the impact of a full night's sleep on the human body, that she awoke refreshed and renewed the next morning. She had slept through the night and devoured a tin of sweet corn as her breakfast. She resisted the temptation to heave as she scooped the yellow morsels from the can. Familiarity breeds contempt in all things. After her prayers, she began to feel the effect of the food as the energy coursed through her veins, her sinews once more alive.

She had no new insight to offer on her predicament. No cure for the chronic loneliness of being the last survivor and yet even the grey day outside seemed brighter. She rekindled the idea of making a move into the countryside. It was said that the northern wilderness had been hardly touched by the insects. Then they probably said the same thing about the city there.

Feeling the need for routine, she picked up the wind up radio she'd scanned religiously up to a few weeks ago before she'd given up against a wall of static. She wound it and began to creep through the frequencies, looking for anything other than electronic garbage. She moved carefully through the stations to ensure she did not miss anything, searching in the interminable numbers for that wireless message in a bottle.

Her conscience was about to whisper something again when she caught a snippet of music. She dialled back and forth, delicately touching the manual dial so it moved just a fraction. Then, she found it again. It was a violin concerto. It sounded crackly like a vintage record, even skipping a bar in places as a tiny cricket danced on the diamond stylus. She kept it low as it was always the vibrations which attracted them. Luckily, the bass on her wind up radio was hollow and tinny so she felt safe enough to listen.

She had once asked an elderly Imam about heaven. He had answered: *"Have you ever listened to a piece of music or viewed a startling work of art and for a few seconds, been lifted to another place, a complete escape from earth to a form of ecstasy."* She remembered giggling at the word. *"This is heaven child. Allah will only allow you to grasp it for very short time,"* he had explained. As the strings of the unseen violin were joined by a cello, she was shown heaven for the second time in her life.

The first had been her pilgrimage to the holy city of Mecca.

She sat for several hours, just listening to the sounds of the radio.

When one piece finished, she could hear someone manually changing the record. The unseen DJ carefully slipped the LP from its sleeve, placed it on a record player and clicked to begin. There was a brief pause before the music crackled into life once more. But, there was never a single word spoken. The end of days radio station was not one of dialogue, of analysis or comment. It had no survival advice to offer. No national emergency update.

It was resignation. And, thus it played some of humanities finest achievements as a shadow fell over the world of men.

The weak radio signal was at least a connection of sorts for her. This was not a looped computer signal or sterile piped music. She could actually hear the mysterious station master selecting and changing the music. But, he remained silent. She was not alone but her wireless companion was distant and nameless; both mute and dumb.

Alive

It had been a month since the assassin bug attack in the shopping mall and food was becoming scarce, the cupboard peppered with just a few remaining tins of vegetables. She searched the apartments once more, this time with starving eyes. She harvested little of consequence. She would have to go out. Something she had been avoiding for the last few weeks.

She had not grown tired of the classical broadcasts but frustrated at the silence of the DJ. She had heard him shuffle and even cough. She knew it was a man. Apart from that he was a mystery. She longed to make contact, even if only to sit and listen with him as humanity was supplanted in the world.

She did not switch the wind up radio off. She simply waited for its stored energy to exhaust itself and die a natural death. This was the omen she needed to move. With a few days rations left, if she didn't forage now, she may not have the strength to go out again. She went into her bedroom and changed from the stained pyjamas she'd been in for days. Looking in the mirror, she realised she'd let herself go. She was now a gaunt and pallid creature. Her young breasts sagged and her eyes were ringed in dark shadows. With precious little water for washing, she'd been quick to abandon her daily cleaning routine.

She opened the wardrobe and took a pair of frayed blue jeans. She forced them on and grabbed a brown leather jacket. She didn't bother locking the door to the apartment, only carefully setting the latch so she could tell if anything had entered her world. A city without people is a city without thieves. The early months of the bio-crisis had been a dark festival of looting, theft and murder. Humans without order, it seemed, were vicious animals.

She had always been told that Allah had written morality into humans. A source code offered by the creator which would guide mankind, be he in the deserts of Arabia or deep space. That was the theory. In harsh reality, she had seen the face of man and it was untrustworthy and violent. Perhaps it was these events which had finally confirmed Allah's decision to cleanse the earth of humanity.

We had the chance for redemption, to help each other and those too weak to survive alone. But, instead, she had truly seen the face of man. Children abandoned in the street or traded for food. Violent and sadistic rapes in broad daylight. She had walked by, fearful for her own safety. Everyone had walked by in the failing light of mankind. Cruel, perverted and squalid. Such was the glorious end to the world. She packed up her kit and prepared for another foraging run. She set the traps as she left the building via the back door. The delicately balanced cans, the taut string and the carefully placed weights. She was paranoid about this ritual every time she went out. She wanted to know who or what might have been in her home whilst she was away. It was a practice that had kept her alive whilst the others laid dead.

She headed out of the backdoor and over the wall into an alleyway polluted with rubbish. She caught sight of a wild dog at the end but it quickly scampered away, leaving waste and paper littering the narrow path. Every yard or so she stopped and listened, holding her breath, to check for the tell-tale click that meant carnivorous attackers were near.

There is no safe place to walk in a world dominated by insects. "Walk in the middle and you risk something jumping from a roof and digging a pointed proboscis into you. Death might be quick but the agony of a few seconds can seem like a lifetime of pain." She heeded her own advice. Words and wisdom passed on from human survivors long since gone. She'd seen them all; army types, amateur survival preppers, armchair warriors. They were dead. She was alive. For all she knew, she and the silent radio person were the only survivors.

She moved slowly through the streets towards an office building near the main square. A huge sprawling concrete affair with a tall imposing tower. It was a design clearly from the 60s. When men ruled the world and their tiny bricks made them feel like gods. Made them feel like they could touch Allah.

She walked past several burnt out homes, watching fearfully for any sign of movement within. Being outside was a dangerous but unavoidable activity. There were simply too many vectors of attack and two eyes could not compete with compound vision.

Her hike was uneventful. The city she saw was still a dead one. Here and there was evidence that the body had been moved but it was still a corpse. Reaching the office complex, she walked through the doors, now empty of their glazed plates. Her target was the upper floors. She looted the ground floor a few weeks ago and the noises from the basement were a black portent of what laid in wait in the darkness there.

Others

The boy with blonde hair led the way as the long convoy behind him snaked off into the distance. Every now and then he would dart into a building, emerging after a few minutes to either continue moving on or tap the wooden stick he was carrying on the ground until a worker ant broke away from the formation and entered.

This routine was repeated as the convoy moved along, broken only by the emergence of a heavily laden ant which would leave the front of the column and trek off down the middle, struggling with items secured from the site.

The girl with dark hair stood back from the window in the towering office block, her mind a tempest of changes. The new world, the one in which the insects had inherited the earth was in question. Here she had witnessed man and insect working together. Peering slowly from her high vantage point, she noticed the boy with the blonde hair directing the ants.

A human controlling an insect?

And people, so many people; the boy with blonde hair, a lady with a walking stick, a crowd in grey jumpsuits – more people than she had seen in months.

She felt the huge burden of carrying the weight of a species' survival on her shoulders dissipate but at the same time, she was flooded by the loneliness of her long isolation. Believing that much of humanity had perished only enforced her loneliness. She had not been a willing participant in it. The horror had been forced upon her. Now there was a choice. For the first time in many months, she could run to them, even join them. Would they welcome her?

As the convoy moved forward and paused below her, she witnessed a man with blue trainers running into the very building in which she was concealed. As he did, several ants waited patiently outside. Waited for their human partners to return. She couldn't imagine what they were after. It was a tall, 15 storey tower block. There was no food here.

She remained calm as the man in blue trainers was absent from her view. She was 11 floors up in a small corner office. At most, these searches seemed to last a few minutes. There was little chance of her being discovered. She shrank back into the shadows and watched the convoy through an open window. A cool breeze brushed her face. It was one of those windows which only allowed her to open it a couple of inches. So fearful were the designers that the long dead workers would hurl themselves to the concrete below that they built this measure into all the windows. It all seemed pointless to her now. After everything that had happened, it wasn't ghoulish to suggest that death by falling from a tower block was infinitely preferable to death at the hands of the insects.

The man with the blue trainers re-emerged into the dull sunshine. He waved the ants on and the lumbering convoy continued. If she did not declare herself to them now, they would be gone. If she did not follow them, she may never come across them again.

Was this the future? Humans and insects working together? Or was it some cruel and inhuman unholy alliance. In their defence, the people looked well-fed and none were chained or bound. These were no slaves.

In a few seconds, she decided her fate. There was little hope in her surviving alone for years to come. This was not a future she either wanted or was prepared for. A yearning for children lingered in the cornered recess of her mind, silent until now, only to ignite on contact with others like dry season kindling to a flame.

She turned and left the office, heading through a fire door into the office block stairwell. It was pitch black as she slowly moved down the stairs, listening for the click clack of an arachnid. These spindly beasts would often set up in dark, lonely places. The smaller arachnids mainly ate birds and smaller mammals but still had crippling toxic bites. She pushed thoughts of the larger arachnids from her mind. These were the true creatures of nightmares. They would rush forward to deliver a bite, only to scramble back and wait for their shocked prey to freeze under the influence of their neurotoxin. Death was not quick. Being eaten alive could last for days. She told herself that the unfortunate humans captured by these creatures could not feel anything. That they were not themselves. It was a good self-deception and one which guarded her sanity.

By the time she reached the bottom of the stairs and emerged from the grey tower block, the convoy was hundreds of yards away. She walked after it, feeling vaguely ridiculous, like a small child chasing the travelling circus as it lumbered through town. Suddenly one of the humans at the back of the column turned and clocked her. The man had only one arm but raised it in acknowledgement. She paused for a few seconds then waved back.

The convoy continue to move but the man with one arm stayed behind, waiting for her to catch up. He snatched glimpses at her but always seemed to turn his face when she looked directly at him. From the back, his hair was a greasy tangle of string, his clothes patched and re-torn. But, he continued to signal to her. Come closer, he seemed to be saying, come closer.

She had no reason to doubt him. She could still have run away and lived out her days alone. When she paused, the man with one arm gave no indication that he would follow or give chase. Finally, she heard him.

"Come and join us," he croaked. He repeated the phrase several times. Perhaps they were picking up lonely survivors in every part of the ruined city. Perhaps there were thousands out there just like her, jealously guarding their isolation and their survival. She continued to walk close but as she did the man with one arm bent over in a fit of coughing, spitting out mucus and bile onto the floor. She opened her mouth to speak but after so long, no noise came from her dry and parched throat.

Her instinct was to rush forward, for she now saw that he was an elderly man. A grey and crooked figure, something she had not seen for many months. Few of the infirm, disabled or elderly had survived the first savage months of the insects.

"Are you OK?" she asked, calling to him. He beckoned her closely and she pulled a bottle of water from her backpack to offer to the stranger.

As she held out the water, he pulled himself upright and for the first time she saw the man with one arm's face. He was an old man but also a curious one, with hues of green around his face, encircling it like the frame of a canvas. He seemed to heave again as if about to vomit but instead, he opened his mouth in her direction and spewed a cloud of tiny green spores, which, like a verdant spray, covered her, soaking into her skin and eyes. She managed to close her mouth in time but the minute droplets were everywhere and there was no escape.

"Come and join us," he whispered before surrendering to another fit of coughing and heaving. She rubbed her eyes.

"What've you done to me?!" she screamed. Others in the convoy turned for an instant then turned back.

She felt a cloud descending over her mind, misting her imagined route back to the apartment and hazing her decision-making. If it was poison, she needed to get somewhere safe and quickly. She tried to keep calm, to stop the rate of circulation but her heart was pumping like a night club bass, infected blood rushing into every artery and vein. The cloud fell over her eyes and all she saw was milky white. A voice through the infectious snow said calmly, "take my hand now." She felt a dry, leathery hand in hers, the fingers wrapping around her. The hand led her away. She had neither the will nor the energy to resist and allowed herself to be led by the man with one arm. She was not alone.

"The blindness will fade," whispered the man with one arm. As the days passed, she left the side of the man with one arm and walked alongside the worker ants as the search of the city continued.

Her eyesight much improved and itchy lichen patches grew on her legs as they did on all of the humans and insects, and she thought of nothing. She witnessed other survivors and learnt the same process the man with one arm had used on her. At the sight of another human, her gut would bulge and gurgle, it was like having a ball of vomit and controlling the instinct to just heave was something she needed to learn. Not only did every human survivor respond to the green spores, so did every insect and not that she noticed, every ant in the column had the same green patches of mould. The only ones uninfected were the arachnids but they stayed hidden. Even through the dullness, she could sense the immense pressure of the fungal growth within her skull but it did not occupy her.

Where insects had surpassed man, it seemed that

they had inherited the throne of the earth. But Allah rarely reveals his great works in one season and so whilst the species gap left by man was filled, or rather taken by insects, so their reign was to be a short and painful one.

For there are things on and below earth which strive also for daylight. And so, the new age of fungus begins. And at the vanguard of the wave is the girl with dark hair.

bed of crimson joy

I

"Are you sure this is a good idea?" said Stanley, scratching at his grey hair and inspecting the bits of scalp under his fingernails.

His spectacles were perched on the end of his nose, giving him an expression halfway between a squint and a sneer. He was wearing his baggy fawn cardigan and tartan slippers.

For a second, Rose wondered if it was a good idea. Stanley wasn't cutting a dashing figure. "Stop being such a fusspot and come on," she said, turning the key in the back door.

"You're only watering the plants and feeding the cat," said Stanley. "I really don't see why you need me here."

"Just get inside will you." She gave him a push and he stumbled through the door into the utility room. Their neighbours had moved in seven months ago, and had already made extensive renovations.

"That's solid corian," Stanley said, running his fingers along a worktop. "Nice work too." Rose walked through to the kitchen shaking her head. She'd forgotten that

Stanley hadn't been inside since Samantha and Darren moved out.

Naturally he'd want to do all those male things, like inspecting the carpentry and admiring the quality of the materials. She'd have to finish her chores quickly or she'd lose him altogether to his inspection of the new kitchen suite.

That wasn't the reason she'd brought him next door. Even if he hadn't realised yet. Rose sighed, she'd always been the one to take the lead in these matters. A momentary pang of regret welled up inside her. Regret for all the things she'd never had from her relationship.

She wanted to be needed, physically. She wanted a man who would chase her, wherever she led him. A man who would just take her, without Rose having to orchestrate the whole thing and lead him through it step by step.

But she was old now. Available men were thin on the ground and she did still have Stanley. He wasn't a passionate husband, but she didn't have much to complain about. Mainly the minor quirks and irritations any long term marriage has to accommodate. Heaven knows, he put up with enough of hers.

"Are you finished yet?" said Stanley, hovering in the kitchen door. The cat eyed the food she'd put out with suspicion. Rose could never work out if the cat hated the food or just the fact that Rose put it out for her.

"I just have to do the orchids," Rose said. Stanley glanced around the kitchen at the new range cooker and the expensive oak cabinets. "Nice what they've done in here," he said. "They obviously have a bit of money."

"Hmm," said Rose, spritzing the orchids with water. She didn't want to encourage too much interest in the new kitchen.

"Right, well I'll be getting back while you finish that off," said Stanley.

"But you've only just got here."

"I've seen all I need to."

"What on earth do you want to go back home for?"

"The snooker's on in a minute, I don't want to miss it."

"But you haven't followed the snooker in ages."

"I caught a few matches on the iPlayer and got back into it."

"Well you can watch the next one on the iPlayer then."

"It's not the same as watching it live."

Rose let out a short, exasperated breath. She started to question the whole thing. It was just like Stanley to spoil everything before he even realised what was on offer. "There's something I want to show you upstairs," she said.

"We can't go up there."

"Why ever not?"

"Because it's not our house. They gave you the keys. I don't even know if they want me in the kitchen, let alone upstairs. It's not right."

"It can't do any harm. They'll never know."

Rose put her head to one side, tilted her hips and shot Stanley a knowing look. It was a look she'd first given him on Boscastle Beach, back in 1970. A look he recognised straight away.

"Oh," he said, and swallowed audibly, making his adam's apple bob. The look was enough to silence him.

Rose took him by the hand and led him up the stairs. He wore the same shocked, yet acquiescent, expression he'd worn forty years ago.

Up until that moment, on Boscastle Beach, Rose had thought Stanley was being a gentleman, out of some antiquated notion of chivalry and respect. She learned, when she seduced him, that fear and inexperience had held him back.

She wished later that she hadn't chosen such a perfect spot for their first tryst. The act itself had been clumsy and embarrassing, and altered Rose's feelings about the secluded cove. She could never recall the location without a sense of awkwardness and regret.

At nineteen she'd been in awe of Stanley's intellect and his talent as a poet. He was only twenty-three when Rose met him and already his poems had been published in several small journals. One of the journals was even stocked by her university's library. She hadn't entirely liked the poems, but she'd admired his achievement. He was the first person in her social circle to be published.

Sadly, as a poet, Stanley had not made good on his early promise. He had improved as a lover, but he'd never quite gotten over the shift in power that sex brought to their relationship. He was threatened by Rose's sexual experience.

Stanley tried to compensate for his inferiority by subtly belittling Rose with his intellect. He wouldn't stoop to an outright insult. He did it all through inference and allusion. Because she recognised the source of his hostility, and because she loved him, Rose had learned to ignore the barbed comments and the subtle taunts.

Rose led Stanley across the landing to the spare room. Stanley was still taking in the reclaimed floorboards and the Farrow and Ball paint that had replaced the flock wallpaper, as Rose opened the door.

"So," she said, making a grand gesture. "What do you think?"

"What do I think of what?"

"Oh come on," she patted the mattress of the king sized, four poster bed that dominated the room. "What do you think I'm talking about?"

The four poster bed took up most of the available space in the room. Rose had no idea how Peter and Bethany had gotten it in there. It was too big to go up the stairs or through the door, or even for them to have winched it through the window.

It was a tudor style canopy bed, with intricately carved oak posts. A nymph and a satyr chased each other round the dark antique wood of the posts. The carved panels of the headboard depicted an obscene bacchanal, in which few of the sexual positions seemed physically possible. The bedspread and curtains were made of a deep red material with gold brocade stitching, decorated with an intricate crest made up entirely from genitalia.

"Oh it's the bed," said Stanley. "That's what you wanted to show me." He looked relieved, like a schoolboy who's been let off a scolding. "I thought... well, I mean, when you... anyway, I've seen it now. Come on, we'd better be going."

"Hold on, I'm not finished yet." Rose pulled herself up

onto the bed and patted the mattress next to her. "Come join me."

Stanley looked more than a little hesitant. "Look Rose, this isn't right. We don't even know Peter and Bethany. We should be getting along now."

Rose sighed with exasperation. The bed was already starting to affect her. All she needed to do was to get Stanley to touch it.

She remembered the first time she saw the bed, when she popped over yesterday. She'd fed the cat and watered the plants and decided to have a nosey about. She got a delicious, clandestine thrill being in someone's house when they were away. It was like sharing an intimate slice of their everyday life, without them knowing.

After checking the cupboards, the bookshelves and the broom cupboard, and finding nothing of any note, Rose decided to head upstairs. The idea of checking the bedrooms gave her a little frisson, especially when she considered the things that might occur there, but they were disappointingly tasteful and bland.

Then Rose walked into the spare room and saw the bed. This was just the sort of secret she'd been hoping to unearth. The bed looked as though it had been waiting for her. She was appalled and fascinated by the carvings and the motif on the spread. Peter and Bethany seemed so prim and self-contained. She knew there had to be something lurking beneath their respectable facade, but she hadn't expected anything so exciting as this.

In the back of her mind she told herself it was time to go back downstairs and leave, she'd pried enough, and she still had to make Stanley's supper. She didn't listen though. Instead she went over to the bed and ran a hand over the spread. A static charge seemed to crackle up her arm. She didn't feel it in her body so much as her emotions, which gave it more force. Her breathing became quick and shallow and her heart beat faster.

The mattress was high and Rose had to pull herself up on to it. She felt a twinge from her bad hip as she swung her leg up. Rose cursed, and shifted her buttocks to ease the pain. She lay on her back and stared up at the tapestry on the underside of the canopy. It showed a naked woman, with large breasts, easing herself onto a large, erect phallus. The anatomical detail of the woman's labia, as they parted to accommodate the huge shaft of the phallus, was very graphic.

Rose was filled with a sudden yearning to be penetrated by such a huge phallus. To feel it, hard and swollen, pumping furiously inside her.

She slipped her hand down the front of her trousers and lifted the frayed elastic of her knickers. Her fingers searched out her clitoris. Rose could not remember the last time she'd done this. She felt out of practice, lacking both the dexterity and the rhythm she needed to please herself.

Then she looked up at the tapestry again and projected herself into the woman's position, imagined lowering herself onto such a magnificent cock and her fingers began to work their old magic.

The orgasm seemed to come from somewhere deep inside the bed. It seeped into her, moving down her thighs and up her spine, lighting up each of her nerve endings. She arched her back, knowing she'd pay for that in the morning but caring not a bit, and let out a moan that became a sob as her whole physique surrendered to the pleasure of coming.

When she was done, Rose lay panting on the bed. She brought her fingers up to her lips and tasted herself. Something she hadn't done since she was a teen, experimenting with personal pleasures. She was pleasantly surprised to find that, despite being long past her menopause, she still loved the taste of her own juices.

She wanted to feel those juices now. She'd gotten Stanley this far, he just needed one last little push.

"Do you think these posts were carved by hand?" she said. "Or one of those carving machines?"

"A router you mean?"

"Yes one of those, what do you think?"

"How on earth should I know?"

"Well, you're the expert. You have such a good eye for these matters. You know so much more than me."

Stanley went to examine one of the posts. Stroking his ego always worked. "I doubt you could get this detail with a router. Plus it's most likely an antique, they wouldn't have had the technology back then."

"Are you sure?"

"Just look at this finish, and the grain of the wood. This has to be done by hand. See how smooth it is."

Stanley ran his hand along the post and Rose smiled. He looked down at the front of his trousers with surprise. A huge bulge had appeared. He looked over at Rose, and she nodded, reaching out a hand to him as she threw back the covers.

For the first time in their marriage, Stanley didn't

need to be led to the bed, didn't need to be guided and gently encouraged. He leaped on Rose.

She tore off his checked flannel shirt and tugged at his thermal vest while he fumbled with his belt.

"Just let me get my glasses off," Stanley said, as Rose tried to wrestle the vest over his head. Rose slipped off her blouse and skirt then pulled off her knickers. She was so excited she didn't even mind that Stanley hadn't noticed they were new.

Her bra was relatively new too. She was about to unclip it when she thought better of it. Better to keep an air of mystery, or at least let Stanley remember her breasts as they used to be. Not as the saggy things they were now.

Stanley was down to his Y-fronts and his socks. One was tartan and one was navy blue. Rose chose to ignore them. She pushed him onto his back, knelt next to him and removed the slightly stained brown and beige Y-fronts.

Stanley sprang free, his erect penis jutting expectantly from a little nest of grey pubic hair. Rose bent and took him in her mouth. He hadn't washed that morning, and he had an old man's musty scent, but he throbbed with appreciation beneath her lips and tongue. A drop of pre-cum trickled over her tongue and Rose felt herself moisten in anticipation.

Stanley groaned and Rose took him out of her mouth. She sat astride him and guided him into her. Rose closed her eyes and pictured the tapestry above her head. As Stanley filled her, she imagined herself as the woman, being taken by the giant phallus.

Rose began to grind her hips. She opened her eyes and caught Stanley's gaze. They smiled furtively at each other, reveling in the forbidden pleasure of fucking in a neighbour's bed.

Peter and Bethany would never expect such a thing. To them, Rose and Stanley were quaint and sexless. An older couple who lived next door. Someone with whom they exchanged Xmas cards and polite greetings in the driveway. People whom they pitied and patronised for their lower income and aging bones.

They certainly weren't the sort of people Peter and Bethany would imagine rutting like animals on their freshly laundered linen the minute they went off on holiday.

When they were done, Rose lay next to Stanley toying with the hairs on his chest. They were so perfectly white Rose imagined them the ghosts of hairs that once lived on Stanley's chest.

"What are you thinking about?" Rose asked him. Stanley chuckled, his mouth set in a supercilious smile.

"I was thinking of Betjeman, and his poem - 'Late-Flowering Lust'."

"Do I want to hear this?"

Stanley ignored her and began to intone:

> "I cling to you inflamed with fear
> As now you cling to me,
> I feel how frail you are my dear
> And wonder what will be—

> "A week? or twenty years remain?
> And then—what kind of death?
> A losing fight with frightful pain
> Or a gasping fight for breath?

"Too long we let our bodies cling,
We cannot hide disgust
At all the thoughts that in us spring
From this late-flowering lust."

Rose rolled over on her side, with her back to Stanley. She blinked away the tears she didn't want him to see. For all his learning, Stanley suddenly seemed very old, yet very childish in his spite.

II

Three days later, Peter and Bethany came home and Rose returned their keys, posting them through the letterbox in an old brown envelope. She'd put the incident with Stanley from her mind, trying her best to forget it.

Rose was frying pork sausages for dinner when there was a loud rap at the front door. It was Peter; despite his tan, and his expensive pink polo shirt, he seemed deeply rattled. His long, thin face was ashen and he looked genuinely appalled about something.

"Peter," Rose said, tucking some loose hairs behind her ear. "How was your holiday?"

"What...? Oh, my holiday, yes my holiday... it was fine thank you."

Peter breathed out heavily through his nose and looked at the floor. He put his hand on the back of his neck and shook his head.

"Look, there's no... erm, easy way to say this. But... well... just what do you think you were you doing in our spare room?"

A cold wave of panic washed over Rose. How could he possibly know. There was no conceivable way. She had laundered all the sheets, put everything back as it was. There was no trace of their passion left in the room.

"I'm not sure I know what you're talking about," she said, trying to hide how dry her throat suddenly felt.

"Oh come on, it's not something you'd miss, is it?"

"I'm afraid you've got me at a loss Peter... I don't, I mean... I simply watered the plants and fed the cat like you asked. I didn't go anywhere near the spare room"

"What I want to know is how you got it up in the first place."

Rose almost gasped. Her shoulders went back and her brow furrowed with indignation. "I don't think I care for your tone Peter. Now, if you'll excuse me I have something on the stove."

Rose started to close the door but Peter blocked it with his hand. "Look, I'm just trying to make sense of it all. I'm not even really that cross, just perplexed. I don't understand how you got it through the door or even up the stairs. Did you get some men in? Was it delivered while we were away? Did you have to sign for it or something?"

"Peter, I'm sorry, you really aren't making any sense. Did we have to sign for what?"

"The bed of course, the ruddy great bed in the spare room."

"Wasn't that already there?"

"So you've seen it. You do know what I'm talking about."

"I might have glimpsed it."

"But I thought you said you didn't go anywhere near the spare room?"

"I had to get the cat down from upstairs at one point."

"The cat's not allowed upstairs."

"Exactly, so I… must have… chased her up there and caught a glimpse of it through the doorway. It's quite noticeable."

"I'll say it's bloody noticeable." Peter stared at her intently. Rose could tell he suspected she wasn't being entirely frank, but that wasn't the biggest of his worries. "So you really have nothing to do with it being there? Because it wasn't there when we left and you're the only person who's been in the house."

"Peter, I hardly know you and Bethany. Why would I put a bed in your spare room while you were away? I'm an old woman and Stanley's plagued by his back. How could we get a four poster bed up those stairs?"

"You didn't pay someone else to do it then?"

"Why would we? We live on a pension. We've got better things to do with our savings than waste them on senseless practical jokes and expensive furniture."

"You didn't see anything suspicious while we were away. No one else calling round with deliveries or something."

"No, not a thing."

"You would tell me if you had seen something, wouldn't you?"

"Of course."

Peter shook his head and stared at the floor, trying to puzzle it all out. "It just doesn't make any sense." He looked up and stared Rose straight in the eye. "No one's threatening you are they? To keep quiet about all this I mean. You can tell me if they are."

"Peter, listen to yourself."

Peter stared up at the window of the spare room next door. Then he turned to go without saying a word of thanks or goodbye. Rose had the distinct feeling she'd been dismissed.

The sausages were burned black when she got back to the kitchen and she had to open a tin of beans instead. Her hands were shaking so much it took two attempts to get the lid off.

She thought at first it was from the confrontation with Peter. When she considered it however, she realised it was the bed that had shaken her. The mysterious bed that had seduced her and Stanley. The four-poster bed that hadn't been in the spare room when Peter and Bethany left for their holiday, but had somehow been waiting, just for her.

III

Late next afternoon, Rose saw workmen carrying chunks of carved wood and a mattress out to a skip in next door's drive. She recognised some of the carvings and the designs on the fabric that the men slung in the skip.

At the end of the day a truck came and took the skip away. Peter and Bethany probably paid a premium to get such prompt service.

Rose was surprised by how upset she felt about the disposal of the bed. It was an antique after all and probably one of a kind. It was wanton vandalism to hack it to pieces and dump it in a skip. It made her wonder what sort of people Peter and Bethany were to treat a rare object like the bed with such violent disregard.

Rose had let go of any foolish thoughts she had about the strange power of the bed. She and Stanley had just indulged in a foolish and uncharacteristic moment of madness that was all. A brief attempt to recapture their youth and deny the stifling hand of age. She was rather embarrassed by the whole incident now, as enjoyable as it had been.

Stanley hadn't looked her in the eye since. He'd retreated into his private world of snooker and DIY catalogues. Rose knew that he felt just as foolish and blamed her for it. It was childish of him, she knew, but he'd get over it if she gave him a bit of time and space.

She didn't suppose that Peter or Bethany would ask her to look after the property next time they went away. She didn't mind too much about this. There were too many memories in the house for her. The extensive renovations hadn't dulled the impact of those memories.

When Darren and Samantha lived there, Rose had been round at least twice a day. Their young children, Paul and Emily, had loved Rose and she was always babysitting and baking them treats. Rose would often have the kids after school once Samantha started work again, to allow her and Darren could keep up with the mortgage.

She and Stanley hadn't been able to have children, though Rose would dearly loved to have been a mother. They tried for a long time but it never happened. Rose had wanted to see a doctor but Stanley wouldn't agree.

He felt it was a personal thing that should be kept between the two of them. He didn't want to go sharing these sort of problems with a stranger, even if that stranger was a trained professional.

In truth, Rose knew that Stanley suspected the problem was with him, and he didn't want that medically confirmed. He already had enough hang ups about his sexuality and Rose didn't want to make him feel any more insufficient.

Stanley turned to poetry to cope with the erosion of his confidence. For a while he was more prolific than he was when Rose first met him. He even placed a couple of the poems with prestigious publications. One of the poems he showed Rose ended with the line:

"Her womb was an instrument of revenge."

She wasn't entirely sure what that meant, but she knew he was subtly taunting her. Turning his inadequacy into hostility towards her. Making it all her problem. It was typical of Stanley to use his intelligence and learning to goad her in such a way that he remained above reproach, while Rose was made to feel insufficient because of her lesser intellect.

As the years drew on, Rose felt increasingly hollowed out by her broodiness. A deep yearning would chip away at her insides every time she saw a pregnant woman. Whenever she heard a small child call out 'Mummy' in a supermarket, Rose's own need to be called 'Mummy' would echo round her hollow interior like a cry of anguish in a canyon.

On her fifty first birthday, Rose stopped bleeding altogether. The ticking of her biological clock had been silenced, once and for all, by the menopause. She crawled into the bath with a bottle of red wine and tried to drown the emptiness with which she was swollen. The mocking emptiness that had eaten the life Rose longed to feel inside her.

Samantha had instinctively known this of course and, while they were good friends, she didn't mind exploiting it, not when it meant endless free child care. When Darren left her, quite unexpectedly, for a younger woman he'd met at work, Samantha relied on Rose even more to help with the children.

That's when the problems started. As Samantha fell apart and was unable to cope, Paul and Emily came to depend more and more on Rose for their everyday parenting. When Samantha started to recover, she began to resent this. Rose was only trying to help, but the closer Paul and Emily got to her, the more Samantha hated her.

"You're not their mother," Samantha had screamed in her face, the last time Rose had seen her. "They're not your children, you can't take my place!"

Rose had simply come round with the schedule for the school's parent teacher meetings. She had offered to drive Samantha there because her car was being repaired, and to wait for them if need be. Samantha had slammed the door in her face.

A month later they moved out and put the house on the market. Samantha didn't leave a forwarding address, nor did she bother to say goodbye.

Paul got in touch with her on Facebook for a while. Rose was overjoyed to hear from him and to find out how he and Emily were getting along. As soon as Samantha found out however, she blocked Rose and threatened her with a restraining order if she ever got in contact with the children again.

A long period of grieving followed for Rose. She was mourning not only the end of her relationship with Paul and Emily, but all her hopes of motherhood. She would never get to comfort or nurture them, or any child, again. She would never see them fall in love for the first time, go off to university, get married or bring home their own first born child for her to see.

The emptiness that filled Rose made it so easy for people to get inside her. And when they did, something deep within her always died.

IV

The next morning Rose was violently sick. She woke feeling nauseous and only just made it to the bathroom before emptying her stomach.

By lunch time she felt fine and put the vomiting down to a fleeting tummy bug. Her stomach was quite painfully bloated though, and the front of her pants felt tight and restricted. She sighed at the thought that her waist was growing once again and she'd probably have to let out all her clothes.

Rose opened the fridge to decide what to have for lunch. As she scanned the contents for inspiration, she was gripped with a sudden desire for pilchards and pickled gherkins. She hadn't had either for over a decade. She had no idea where the desire came from, but Rose could already taste them. Her mouth watered and her stomach rumbled its appreciation. They weren't foods she liked, but the need to eat them was overwhelming, as though the oily fish and sour vegetables would instantly fix everything that ailed her.

The next morning she woke just as nauseous and brought up everything she'd eaten the night before. There were no more problems for the rest of the day, other than a severely bloated stomach and a few odd cravings.

This pattern continued for the next few days. The doctor told her it was nothing to worry about, probably just a bug. "Come and see me in a few days time if the symptoms continue," she said, without looking up from her computer. "I'll give you some pills for the nausea." Rose had waited for over an hour and the appointment lasted less than three minutes.

The symptoms did continue, though Rose didn't bother to return to her doctor. The bloating got so severe all Rose could wear was a pair of old leggings and her sweatpants.

She stood in front of the mirror in their bedroom, about a fortnight after the nausea started, and stared at her gut. It was noticeably protruding now. She looked like a famine victim with a distended belly, except she wasn't malnourished, despite the early morning vomiting.

Stanley, who was already in bed, looked up from his book and saw her stroking her belly.

"How Blakean," he said.

"What?"

> "Oh Rose thou art sick,
> The Invisible Worm
> That flies in the night
> In the howling storm:
>
> "Has found out thy bed
> Of crimson joy:
> And his dark secret love
> Does thy life destroy."

Rose turned and glared at Stanley with such venomous fury that the smug grin dropped from his face. He looked shocked and a little scared. Like a guilty schoolboy who's just been overheard using bad language. He blinked, swallowed and went back to his book.

V

A week later they were just settling down to watch *Masterchef* when there was a loud rapping on their door. Rose got out of her armchair and winced at the pain in her lower back. Stanley stood and placed a gentle hand on her shoulder.

"You sit yourself down love," he said gently. "I'll get it."

Rose patted his hand and sank back into her chair with a painful sigh. Stanley was worried about her health. The early morning vomiting had stopped, but her stomach had really swollen. It was heavy and painful.

Stanley wanted to call the doctor, but after the last debacle Rose wasn't keen to go back.

"Peter?" Rose heard Stanley say in the hallway, followed by the sound of Peter barging in. "Why don't you come in?" Stanley continued as Peter marched into the living room.

Rose got to her feet to greet Peter, holding her stomach. There were dark bags under Peter's eyes. His clothes were rumpled, his hair hadn't been combed, he needed a shave and there was alcohol on his breath.

"Have you seen her?" he said. "Has she been in touch?"

"Have we seen who Peter?" Rose said. Peter looked irritated by the question, as though Rose was stupid for asking.

"Bethany of course," he said. "She's disappeared. Has she called round or been in touch with you?"

"No, I haven't seen her in days. When was the last time you saw her?"

Peter stared at Rose with disbelief, as though he couldn't believe she could ask such a question. Then he shook his head and stared at the carpet, massaging his temples with his left hand.

"We went to bed last night, same as normal. I woke up this morning and she was gone. I've called everyone I can think of, no-one knows where she is."

"Maybe she just needed to get away from everything," said Stanley. "Sometimes people do. She might even be back later tonight."

Peter turned to look at Stanley for the first time. Regarding him with such withering disdain that both Stanley and Rose frowned.

"You don't understand," Peter said. "We were in the bed."

"Isn't that where people usually are first thing in the morning?" said Rose.

"Not in bed. In the bed. The one we got rid of."

"I'm not following you Peter."

"We went to bed last night in our usual bed. The one that cost a fortune from John Lewis. When I woke up this morning I was in the four poster. Our old bed was gone and the four poster was in its place, right there, in our bedroom."

"I don't quite see how that's possible."

"Don't you think I know that! Do you know how much I paid to get rid of it the first time? But there it was in our bedroom."

"Was Bethany in the bed with you?"

"Yes... well no. I mean, she was to begin with, I swear she was. I could feel her next to me as I woke. Her back was pressing against mine. I rolled over to spoon, with my eyes still closed, and there was this faint noise, like a hiss or someone wheezing and trying to catch their breath. Then suddenly she wasn't there. The sheets were still warm. I could smell her on them but she was gone, as though she'd just, I don't know... fizzled out."

"Fizzled out?"

"Yes," said Peter, getting annoyed with her. "That's the best way I can describe it, okay? That's what it felt like."

"How are you and Bethany getting on at the moment?" said Stanley.

"What business of yours is that?" Peter retorted.

"Well none really, only, looking at this objectively, the most obvious explanation is that she's probably behind all this."

"What on earth are you talking about?" Peter's voice was frigid with disapproval.

"Well, think about it for a moment. Who is best placed to deliver a four poster bed to your house if not one of the occupants? Someone who knows when you're going to be away. Maybe the second time, she slipped you an incredibly strong sleeping pill, then had the old bed taken away and put you back in the new one before you woke. Perhaps she slipped away just as you were waking, but you didn't see her go because you were still a bit drugged."

"That is the single most ridiculous thing I have ever heard! Why on earth would she want to do that? Why would anyone want to do that?"

"Maybe she's trying to drive you mad. Maybe she wants you out of the way. I don't know, that's why I asked how you were getting on. But how would anyone else manage to deliver two identical beds to your house without at least one of you noticing?"

"But it wasn't two identical beds. It was the same one. The exact same one. That's what I'm trying to tell you."

"It couldn't possibly be the exact same bed." said Rose, in measured tones, trying to calm Peter. "You destroyed the first bed, hacked it to pieces."

"I know, but it keeps coming back. The same bed keeps returning. You couldn't replicate something this unique. The carvings, the curtains, the throws, they're all identical."

"Even the tapestry on the underside of the canopy?" said Stanley. Peter stopped what he was about to say and glared at Stanley with suspicion.

"How do you know there was a tapestry?"

"Well I... I mean I... erm..." Stanley went dead-white and Rose could have throttled him.

"He saw it in the skip, when you threw it out," she said. "I would have thought that was obvious. Such a waste too, it was unique, it must have been worth quite a bit."

"But we didn't throw the tapestry in the skip. We burnt it separately. There's no way you could have known about that tapestry unless you'd been on the bed. You wouldn't have seen it if you'd just looked through the door of the spare room."

Now it was Rose's turn to go white. "That's not the point," she said, trying to gather herself. "Bethany is missing and someone is delivering beds to your house without you knowing. Let's focus on the important issues here."

Peter wasn't listening. He was staring with horror at Rose's belly. He backed away from her shaking his head ever so slightly. "Oh my God," he said. "You didn't, you didn't, you have no idea what you've done, have you?" The back of his legs touched the sofa and he collapsed on to it, like a rag doll someone had tossed onto the furniture. All the life drained from his muscles. He put his head in his hands and began to cry.

Rose and Stanley exchanged a puzzled look. This was not the response they expected. "Go and get some brandy," Rose told Stanley. She sat beside Peter, settling carefully into position to accommodate the weight of her distended belly.

"You don't understand what you've done, do you?" Peter muttered, staring at his lap. "I'm fucked, I'm absolutely fucked."

"Peter, you're not making any sense," Rose said. Stanley returned with a large glass of brandy and Peter sipped it gratefully.

"Peter," Rose said, putting a hand on his arm. "What is it that you think we've done? What don't we understand? Does it have something to do with Bethany's disappearance?"

"It has everything to do with Bethany's disappearance." Peter drained the last of the brandy from the glass. He seemed to be weighing up how much to tell them.

"You have to tell us," said Rose. "It's important."

Peter sighed and handed Stanley his glass for a refill. "The bed, I've seen it before, that is, before I moved here. Bethany and I are lawyers, used to be lawyers. We worked for a firm that specialised in probate and estate management. That's where we met actually. It was against company rules to get involved with other staff, plus Bethany was already married, which made it even more complicated, but we were the best at what we did, so they let it slide.

"Our clients were old and rich, and mainly came to us through personal recommendation. We had one client, though, who was a little eccentric. He was a recluse called Archibald Trelawney. He had a huge personal fortune and a vast property portfolio. When word got out that he was looking to expand his legal team, Bethany and I did everything we could to get an introduction.

"He never left his home, some crumbling, gothic pile in the middle of his country estate, so that's where we went to meet him. We were carefully vetted before we got an introduction, so I have to admit, we were curious and a little excited to finally meet the elusive Mr Trelawney.

"A shame then that he made our flesh crawl. We were shown into this little back room on the ground floor, where he seemed to spend all his time. A poky little space filled with books, lining the walls and sittting in huge piles everywhere. He had a mansion with four wings and acres of land around it, yet he hardly ever left this one room. You could tell by the smell.

"He had these horrid little eyes, sunken into a wizened head. They made you feel dirty just by looking at you. He was well spoken and obviously educated, but he had a way of speaking that made everything he said sound lewd and inappropriate. He smiled the minute he saw us, it was a predator's smile, made you feel someone had rammed an ice pick in your guts.

"We had a pretty slick Powerpoint presentation all prepared, but he wasn't the least bit interested. It turned out he had a proposal all of his own. He didn't beat about the bush or anything, he just came straight out with it. He asked how we'd like to inherit his whole estate, money and all. We thought he was joking, obviously. So we laughed it off and tried to steer him back to employing our company.

"Turns out he was being deadly serious. He wasn't

looking for lawyers, he was looking for a couple – the right couple, and he liked what he saw in us. He offered to make us sole benefactors. With one single stipulation, we had to do something in return. Something quite unorthodox..."

Peter stopped, shook his head in revulsion and got to his feet. "I'm sorry," he said. "I've said too much already." Stanley also stood, to block Peter from leaving.

"Wait," Stanley said. "You can't stop there. You haven't told us anything. This is important."

"Look, I've taken up too much of your time. I shouldn't have come here in the first place, you don't know where Bethany is. I need to get as far away as possible."

Stanley moved in front of the door. "Don't leave please, we need to know what the stipulation was."

"No you don't, you really don't. But I do need to leave. I have some post of yours by the way, the post man delivered it to us by accident. I'll drop it off before I go."

Rose pulled herself off the sofa and put her hand on Peter's shoulder. "Peter, look at me, please. You know something about that bed, about Bethany's disappearance and..." Rose rubbed her stomach. "And about what's happened to me. Stanley's right, this is important to all of us. We won't judge you, we might even be able to help you, but we can't do anything unless we know the whole truth. Please, come and sit down, Stanley will get more brandy."

Peter seemed to waver. Rose motioned for Stanley to refill his glass and took advantage of his indecision, to steer him back to the sofa. Peter accepted the fresh glass of brandy and stared straight ahead of him. "You were going to tell us about the unorthodox stipulation…" Rose prompted.

Peter sighed. "Where do I start? I mean, I'm a man of the world and everything. Some of my richer clients have had some… interesting tastes, but this turned out to be… well… I mean we thought at first it was just a harmless peccadillo.

"He was going to let us inherit everything, so long as we agreed to… to… I can't believe I'm telling you this. So long as we agreed to have sex, in a special bed, in his house, while he was in the room with us. We weren't even sure he was serious when he first put it to us. I mean we'd come there to win his business. We didn't expect to be offered the whole estate if we put on some private sex show for the old pervert.

"We asked for a bit of time to think it over, but the old bastard put the hard sell on us, saying we'd have to give him an answer straight away. Well, what would you have done? I mean he was offering us more money than we could spend in several lifetimes. Naturally we agreed.

"But it didn't stop there, the paperwork we had to sign was incredible. I mean, this was our area of specialty but even we were overwhelmed by it and, because of the nature of the transaction, we couldn't employ anyone to negotiate on our behalf, or help us with the more esoteric parts. A huge part of it was in Latin, which I'm not great on. The problem was, a lot of it dealt with laws that we weren't familiar with, some weren't even laws of the earthly realm, that is to say they… no, I'm not making much sense.

"Anyway, back to the… erm, act we had to commit. We

had to do all these strange exercises for about a month leading up to it. We'd be picked up and driven to the estate and some strange people would instruct us to do some very odd things. They'd give us these hideous herbal concoctions to drink as well, it was all very bizarre.

"Then one night we were taken to this bed chamber on the second floor of the mansion. It had magical symbols, drawn on the floorboards in ash and daubed on the walls in blood. The room was filled with erotic art, statues and paintings, most of it was unspeakably obscene. We nearly bolted when we saw it, in spite of all the cash at stake.

"In the centre of the room was the bed. That's where we were supposed to... perform. It wasn't... it's actually not as easy as... I mean I don't normally have any trouble. I've never fancied anyone like I fancy Bethany, but it was different with him in the room.

"When the old goat saw that I was... I was having trouble, he... No, no I can't tell you..."

Rose put her hand on Peter's shoulder. "This is important, I told you we won't judge, but every little detail might be pertinent."

Peter drained his glass. "He put something up... look you have to understand that I'm not into any of the funny stuff. I'm not gay, or kinky, okay? But he... put something up my behind. A little muslin bag filled with exotic spices. Felt like my arse was on fire, excuse my French, but I don't think I've ever been harder. I didn't have any problem after that and, well, you both know what the bed can do to you.

"When we finished, we heard this weird hissing noise, like someone wheezing or gasping for breath. It was just at the point that I climaxed actually. We looked over at Trelawney and he was slumped over in his chair, dead. A thin trickle of dark green fluid ran from the corner of his mouth. He'd poisoned himself.

"Can't say we were sorry to see the back of the old goat. I mean everything was ours now, or so we thought. The first thing we did was get rid of all the old books and the obscene art, not to mention the furniture and furnishings. We could have sold some of it I suppose, it was all antique, some of the books and the statues were worth quite a bit I'm told, but we were already fabulously wealthy so we didn't need the extra money. Beside I never really went in for antiques. Most importantly though, we got rid of that monstrous bed, or at least we thought we had.

"Then all these notaries started crawling out of the woodwork, especially when Bethany discovered she was pregnant, which kind of surprised us. Bethany had been told she couldn't have children. It was one of the reasons her first marriage broke down, her husband was desperate for kids.

"There were all these clauses in the paperwork we signed, that we either hadn't seen, or hadn't understood. Most of them were to do with the care and provision for any children we might have in the first year of our inheritance. So naturally the first thing we did was lawyer up ourselves, inasmuch as we could, given the paperwork we'd signed, which forbade challenging the terms and conditions of the will under pain of forfeit.

"We also got some Latin scholars to translate the passages we couldn't follow. There was a lot of references to an aeternae ultionis clause, meaning eternal, or unending, vengeance which, if invoked, would result in us being punished over and over and over again. Though it didn't specify how this would be done from a legal perspective, so we weren't too bothered about that.

"What did worry us were our legal imperatives under the rerum tanta novitas clause. This specified our roles in a magical ceremony that we had no idea we were taking part in. A ceremony to incarnate a grown man inside the womb of a barren woman, so he'd grow to manhood with all the knowledge and memories of his former life.

"Bethany was pretty freaked out, I can tell you. She didn't like the idea of being pregnant in the first place, she was only three months gone but she looked more like six or seven. It wasn't helping our marriage any either. Then, when she found out about this, it sent her over the edge.

"I mean neither of us believed it was real, not at first. But she knew that something wasn't right with her condition. She said she could feel him growing within her like a tumour, sucking the life out of her. She thought it was like a form of unending rape, having that creepy old goat deep inside her. She even became convinced she could hear his thoughts, goading her and laughing at her from inside her own womb.

"It was driving her mad so we had to do something about it. If that was Trelawney growing inside her, we certainly didn't want to raise him after he was born. Can you imagine that? A little toddler running around with the mind and memories of an evil old man, calling you 'Mummy' and 'Daddy'. Looking into a tiny infant's eyes and seeing that malevolent old fossil staring out of them. I can't think of anything worse.

"We made discreet enquiries about terminating the pregnancy. No one wanted to help us at first, they thought Bethany was too late in her term, because of how big she was. Eventually we found a clinic with questionable ethics and a liking for six figure fees. When it was over we told the solicitors that Bethany had miscarried.

"Unfortunately they followed the money trail to the clinic and exposed our little lie. We lost the whole estate. We'd gone back on our deal and as such we'd forfeited our right to the inheritance. We had to do it though, after the way that bastard had played us. At least we foiled his little plan."

Rose was suddenly reminded of the line from Stanley's poem: 'Her womb was an instrument of revenge.'

"What did you do then?" Stanley asked.

Peter coughed. "Sorry my throat's dry from talking so much. Don't suppose I could ask for a glass of water?" Rose fetched it this time. Peter smiled his thanks and drank it down. "Well we had to move out. There was a fight about what we owned, the possessions we'd brought to the mansion, the things we bought while we were there. That took a while to resolve. We'd salted a little of the money away where it couldn't be found, so we were okay financially. We moved here to stay under the radar. Then we tried to put everything behind us. We thought we'd succeeded until that wretched bed suddenly turned up."

"What are we going to do?" said Rose. She wasn't quite certain what to make of Peter's incredible confession. Part of her wondered how much of it was fantasy and self-delusion? A fantastical tale invented by someone close to breaking point, in order to cover up a more prosaic case of fraud and embezzlement. Another part of her was reluctantly accepting the truth of it, and how it accounted for all the strange little events that had befallen her.

"I'm going to get as far away as possible from that bed. Then I'm going to find Bethany." He got up from the sofa and made his way out of the room. Stanley didn't attempt to stop him this time. Peter stopped in the doorway, turned to Rose and pointed at her stomach. "You'd be wise to get rid of that as soon as possible."

Stanley followed Peter to the front door and saw him out. Rose stood in the living room with her hands round her swollen belly. It wasn't until Peter's parting comment that she'd even begun to consider there was a life growing inside her.

VI

Rose didn't sleep at all that night. She didn't sleep much these days as it was. Sleep was like an old friend with whom she'd once been close, but had now drifted apart. She only spent a few hours in its company most nights.

Stanley, on the other hand, had become much better acquainted with sleep. He went to bed much earlier, got up later and was always dozing off in the afternoon. He'd also developed a dreadful snore which disturbed Rose's light sleep.

Tonight, she was trying to process everything Peter had said. The implications were too much to take in all at once. She had to let them slowly creep up on her, one at a time, so she could mull each one over and process how she felt.

Rose stared at her huge belly in the dim light of the bedside lamp. She couldn't help stroking it in a proprietary fashion. If Peter was telling the truth, and she suspected he was, then there was something wholly unnatural inside her. The simple fact that she was pregnant, more than a decade after going through the menopause, pointed to how unnatural it was. It had never crossed her mind, or her doctor's, that all the symptoms might add up to this.

Bethany had described it as a tumour, a permanent rape. Peter had advised her to get rid of it as soon as possible. Rose didn't feel like doing that just yet. She knew she ought to be appalled. If Peter was to be believed, she'd been used in the most awful way and had dragged Stanley into it too.

But she didn't feel violated at all. She had what she'd wanted her whole life, another life growing inside her. Rose couldn't believe how quickly she'd come to accept this. It seemed a ridiculous thing to contemplate. Then again, she'd known something wasn't right for a while, somewhere at the back of her mind she'd been preparing herself for this. Given every other strange occurrence of late, it made a sort of twisted sense.

Rose knew that it wasn't right. She knew that soon she would have to rectify the situation. But right now she wanted to enjoy the feeling of being pregnant. Of nurturing another life inside her, of filling the aching hollowness that had screamed at the centre of her being for more than half her life. She liked feeling pregnant. Finally, after all these years, she got to know what it was like.

Rose wondered how someone her age would even go about getting a termination. She supposed she would have to go to some seedy backstreet establishment, which wouldn't be cheap.

Rose weighed up the alternatives to abortion. Would it be possible to get an exorcist to chase Trelawney out of her foetus, if he was actually in there? How about after he was born, would it work better then? She'd read somewhere that a frontal lobotomy could erase unpleasant and troubling memories. Would that work? Could you erase the entire memory of a past life? Would it be possible to perform a lobotomy on a new born child?

The more Rose considered it, the more desperate and brutal each of the alternatives seemed. There was no way she could commit any of them on a child she brought into the world. What were the risks attached to bringing a child to full term at her age? Surely there'd be complications. Given how quickly she was growing, she wondered if she'd even have to carry it for nine months.

As the sky outside her bedroom window began to lighten, Rose began to cry silently. Tears spilling from her cheeks in condemnation of the sheer unfairness of her situation. Here she was with a child – or something like it – inside her, and she would have to kill it. There, she'd said it. Kill it. That's what she was contemplating after all.

She'd brought this on herself. Her longing had drawn this old man into her and now she was expected to kill him. She laughed with a bitter irony. The emptiness that filled Rose made it so easy for people to get inside her. And when they did, something deep within her always died. Literally this time.

Rose ran her hand over her stomach and something moved inside it. Despite everything she'd been thinking, Rose felt a huge burst of excitement. She rubbed the spot where she'd felt the movement, hoping to get more.

That's when she became aware of another consciousness, waiting on the outskirts of her own. One that was rooted to the strange life inside her. It was there at the very edges of her mind, she could sense it more than hear it, like trying to see something hovering in your peripheral vision.

The strongest thing she sensed in this consciousness was need. A need for her, like none she'd ever felt before. Need that came in the form of a plea: please look after me, and love me and raise me. Was this what it meant to be a mother? To be needed this badly and this much.

Beneath the need, other emotions festered, tainting the purity of the need for her. There was cunning, and an ability to manipulate, but there was also a definite sense of threat – you better had look after me.

There was another kick inside her and Rose felt herself flush with pride for the clever little thing in her womb. The consciousness on the perimeter of her own almost seemed to form a thought, a little proto-thought: look what I can do Mummy.

Yes my little darling, she thought, in reply. Show me.

There was more movement, but this time it came with a sharp stab of pain. A pain that kept building until it was beyond agony. It knocked the breath of her, and Rose could only open her mouth in a silent wail of pain.

The skin on her swollen belly began to stretch as something pushed against her from inside. The skin stretched further and she could clearly make out the fingers of a hand. Not a soft fleshy hand. The fingers were gnarled and seemed to be made out of twisted bone and there on the end of them, through the taut skin of her stomach, she could clearly see tiny claws.

VII

Rose was in the garden when the phone went. She was trying to get rid of a particularly stubborn outbreak of bind weed before she got too big to do any more gardening.

She was growing at an alarming rate and had given up any hope of seeing her feet in the near future. This made clambering up off her knees, and shuffling into the house, very uncomfortable.

The answer machine took the call before Rose could get to the phone. She picked up the receiver but the blessed thing kept recording. Like a lot of modern technology, the intricacies of operating it completely defied Rose. She'd bought the thing under protest because her old machine, that she'd had for nearly fifteen years, kept cutting off callers and mangling the tapes she put in it.

"Hello, hello," said Rose, randomly pushing buttons on the machine.

"Oh... hello, is that Mrs Shotton?" said the young man who'd been leaving the message.

"Yes, that's me."

"Hello there, my name's Keith, I'm calling from the Bridge Hotel. Do you know a Mr Peter Hince?"

"Yes, he's my neighbour, why?"

"He's been staying with us recently, but we haven't been able to locate him for the past couple of days. There was some post in his possession that's addressed to you. You haven't seen or heard from him recently have you?"

"No, not for the last couple of weeks. Is anything wrong?'

"Well it's rather hard to explain Mrs Shotton. Would you be prepared to come and collect some of his things? We're not too far from you."

"Erm, I'm not too sure, when would you need me?"

"Whenever you're available Mrs Shotton, but we'd appreciate it if you could come in sometime today or tomorrow."

"And what would you like me to pick up?"

"Again, that's rather hard to explain over the phone, you'd really have to see it for yourself. Shall I expect you later today?"

"Well, okay, I think, but I'll have to check."

"Splendid Mrs Shotton. Would you like me to e-mail you directions?"

"No, that's alright, I'll find you on the map."

"Okay Mrs Shotton, I'll hopefully see you later today, just ask for Keith at reception."

"Okay bye," Rose said and hung up. She felt more than a little coerced into visiting the hotel, but she was curious about Peter. He must have accidentally taken the letters he was going to drop round with him

Two days after Rose last saw him, an estate agent's sign had appeared in Peter's front garden. Rose hadn't seen anyone come to view the house, but a team of cleaners had called round to spruce the place up. Rose hadn't expected to hear from Peter after that, so she was more than a little intrigued by the call from the hotel.

The Bridge Hotel was a shabby, modern building, just off a busy A-road. It was a bland, featureless building with a large gravel forecourt. It looked like a Travelodge or Holiday Inn that had seen better days.

The reception area smelled strongly of air freshener and needed a lick of paint. Rose asked to see Keith and was introduced to a tall, thin man with spiky blond hair and bad skin.

"Mrs Shotton," Keith said. "Thank you so much for coming in." Keith was having great difficulty taking his eyes off Rose's stomach. She supposed it didn't quite gel with her grey hair and crow's feet. It was actually the first time in about three decades that a man hadn't been able to make eye contact with her. Sadly it wasn't her chest that was drawing his gaze, but she thought he could be forgiven, under the circumstances.

"I wonder if you could just sign a few forms for us and then you can pick up Mr Hince's things. Oh, here's your post by the way." Keith held up a few official looking letters in brown envelopes as Rose waddled over to the reception desk.

"What sort of forms?" she said with a little suspicion.

"Oh nothing too important, just some silly legal stuff."

"What kind of legal stuff? I thought I was just doing you a favour by popping by to pick up Peter's things."

"It's nothing major, don't worry. It's just something our legal department said you had to sign."

"Why?"

Rose shifted uncomfortably from foot to foot. Her arches hurt from standing.

"Just so that the hotel is covered legally, when it comes to damages and transportation."

"Well, I brought my car, that's all the transportation we'll need isn't it?"

"Not for everything I'm afraid."

"But surely he just brought a few suitcases."

"Yes, but there is one item that's... shall we say - rather cumbersome..."

"What on earth do you mean?"

"Look, it's a bit hard for me to describe. I think I better show you Mr Hince's room."

Keith took Rose down a series of ground floor corridors towards the rear of the building. The walls were hung with bad watercolours of old cathedrals. The paper was coming away in places and the carpet was well worn.

Keith stopped beside a wood paneled door with chipped white paint. "The thing is," he said, slipping the electric key in the lock, "We have no idea how Mr Hince got this in the room. It wasn't there when he booked in.

We only discovered it after he disappeared. As far as we can tell, he left everything he had in the room, car keys, phone, you name it. We tried everything we could to get hold of him, but he's nowhere to be found. You were our best lead."

Keith opened the door and stepped inside. "You see what I mean. He couldn't have gotten this through the window or down the corridor. No one saw him carry it in the entrance. It's not on the CCTV footage. Where did it come from?"

Keith was standing in the doorway with his back to Rose, so she couldn't see into the room. Nevertheless she knew exactly what he was going to show her before he ushered her inside. The poky little room, scattered with Peter's clothes, was utterly dominated by a four poster bed. Rose felt her stomach lurch as she recognised the carved posts, the bed spread and the obscene tapestry on the underside of the canopy.

"Why would anyone do something like this?" said Keith. "Is it some kind of sick joke? I just don't understand it."

Rose couldn't bring herself to answer Keith. She knew that their efforts to trace Peter's whereabouts would come to nothing. Just as Peter's attempts to find Bethany had been futile.

She felt the unborn creature inside her start to kick at the proximity of the bed. Rose winced and put a hand to her stomach.

"Are you alright?" said Keith.

"Yes, I just felt a kick, I'll be alright in a moment."

"So you are actually... I mean, at your age... is that possible?"

"It came as a great surprise to me."

Rose staggered. At the back of her mind she felt the foetus's brain come to life. Its thoughts seeping into hers like bile leaking from a ruptured spleen. They were half-formed and struggling for comprehension, a still growing consciousness trying to recall something from a former life.

Rose recognised what the unborn life was trying to grasp at though. It was a clause in a contract. Aeternae ultionis, meaning eternal, or unending, vengeance which, if invoked, would result in being punished over and over and over again.

Rose felt her legs go from under her and she sat down hard on the floor. "Is everything okay?" said Keith.

"No," Rose replied. "I've got to go."

"But what about your post, and Mr Hince's things?"

"You can keep them."

"And the bed?"

"Hack it to pieces and burn every single last bit of it."

VIII

"Rose, love, you need medical attention." Stanley was really worried now. He'd been trying to wheedle Rose into seeing a doctor for the past five days. Ever since she retired to her bed.

Her stomach had become so huge that she couldn't carry the weight of it. She was at least twice the size of any normal pregnant woman at the end of her third trimester. Her calf muscles and joints were inflamed, her ankles were swollen and her lower back was pure agony.

Stanley was being ever so sweet to her, for a change. He rearranged her pillows whenever she asked him, brought her soup, and any other food she demanded, and even gave her frequent sponge baths.

As a consequence Rose was being frightful to him. She bullied and berated him at every turn, until he was cowed into submission. And Stanley was so concerned that he took whatever abuse she hurled at him.

"It's not natural love," he said for the fortieth time that day.

"And just what am I going to tell the doctor, if you do call for him? That my husband and I had sex on a magical bed and now I'm pregnant, even though I'm in my sixties?"

"You're not pregnant love, you can't be."

"And why not?"

"Because you're too old and you're too big. No one gets that big when they're pregnant."

"Then what have I got growing inside me?"

"I don't know, a parasite or something, like a tapeworm perhaps. Maybe it's just a bloody big tumour, but it's not a baby. It can't be, it's not possible."

"I can feel him moving inside me. I can hear his thoughts, I know he's there."

"No you can't love, you only think you can. You're not well and you're imagining things."

"I am not imagining things!"

"You are love, and it's bloody well got to stop, right now!"

Stanley pulled his mobile out of his pocket, much to Rose's amazement. It was an ancient, cheap thing she'd bought him from Argos. He drove her mad most of the time because he refused to carry it anywhere and even when he did, he left it turned off so she could never reach him. He must have thought the situation was grave to have actually charged it.

As Stanley began to dial the number, Rose felt a kick. Urgency and alarm emanated from her womb. A voiceless plea burst into her mind. He's going to hurt me mummy. They're going to take me away from you. Please don't let them take me away from you!

Like a lioness whose cub is in danger, Rose felt a wave of murderous anger engulf her. She remembered there was a kitchen knife under her pillow. She'd put it there when she became bedridden, at the insistence of her unborn. She hadn't given it much thought at the time, but now she realised why she'd been prompted to hide it there. Many things she did these days were done unconsciously for the good of her unborn child.

Stanley was still dialing when she rolled off the bed, reared up on her feet and lumbered towards him. The pain in her spine and the back of her legs was almost crippling. If she hadn't been filled with adrenaline and spurred on by homicidal intent, Rose would have collapsed on the floor in agony.

She raised the knife over her head and lunged at Stanley with her other hand. She grabbed his shoulder and they toppled to the ground. Stanley gasped with pain as the air was knocked out of him and Rose's immense weight pinned him to the ground.

The phone fell from his hand. Rose brought the knife down. Stanley yelped with fear. She smashed the point into the phone's screen and shattered it.

Rose brought her face right up close to Stanley's. "You are not doing anything to endanger the life of my baby," she growled.

Stanley whimpered with pain as Rose shifted her weight, crushing his arm beneath her. She rolled off him onto her back and started to push herself back towards the bed with her legs.

Stanley got to his feet, wincing with pain. "Here, let me help you," he said. Rose waved the knife at him.

"Don't you come near me," she shouted, in a deep, ragged voice that sounded nothing like her own and surprised her with its viciousness.

She caught Stanley's eyes. He looked deeply wounded. Unable to believe that she could treat him this way after forty years of marriage.

Part of Rose wanted to reach out to him. To apologise for her manic behaviour, take him in her arms and soothe his hurt. But that part of her was not in charge.

She was not in charge. In that moment Rose realised that her mind was now the consciousness on the periphery, and the iron will of the being inside her womb was in full control of this situation.

"Get out," she screamed. "Get away from me, damn you, go!"

Stanley slunk from the room. His face showed shock and disbelief. His hands were shaking and his shoulders were slumped with dejection.

Rose pulled herself up onto the bed and cried out with the torment from her back. She rolled onto her side to relieve the immense pressure from her swollen front.

Her unborn was still agitated and she stroked her stomach to soothe the both of them.

She lay like this for several hours. Sometime in the early evening she heard Stanley let himself out of the front door. She didn't know where he was going, but she was suddenly seized with the knowledge that it was the last time she would ever see or hear from him again.

Rose began to cry, her body wracked with deep heaving sobs. Her chest swam with regret for all the things she'd had to sacrifice, including her marriage, in order to finally be a mother. She'd had to rid her life of everything that filled it, in order to stop feeling so empty inside.

It's time mummy, her unborn thought, and she knew he was right. She circled his mind like a satellite sentience, sensing his intent from afar, without fully comprehending it.

There was a faint hissing noise coming from far away, rising imperceptibly in volume. The louder it got the more it sounded like someone wheezing and struggling for breath. Rose knew what it was. It was the sound of her former existence, breathing its last.

The sheets beneath her began to change in consistency, coarsening from crumpled cotton to finely pressed linen. She was aware of four objects approaching the bed, as if from a great distance, each with a trajectory that ended on a different corner. As they got closer, Rose saw they were carved wooden posts. A canopy with a tapestry on its underside descended upon the bed as if from a steep height.

Rose was filled a sense of déjà vu, as if she had dreamed all this many times before. Only it wasn't quite something she'd already seen, so much as something she'd already lost. As though her former life, and everything she'd been experiencing until now, was a distant memory that had returned briefly to taunt her with everything she'd forsaken.

Rose looked around her at the four poster bed and the oak paneled room filled with obscene art. She'd never seen its lewd furnishings, or the magical symbols daubed in blood on the walls and formed in ash on the floor. However, she knew exactly where she was.

It begins, thought the life within her womb. And though he had yet to leave her body, Rose had never felt more distant from him, nor more afraid.

IX

Rose had studied every stitch of the tapestry on the canopy. Sometimes, as she lay on her back and looked up at it, she liked to imagine how it was woven, reconstructing its composition. She would picture the weaver working the threads of the weft back and forth through the warp. Working their way up and along the tapestry until it was done. It was a good way to keep her mind off what was happening to her.

The obscenity and eroticism of the image were long since lost on her. She'd been staring up at it for such a length of time it had lost its power to shock. Even so, Rose had no idea how long she'd been on the bed, trapped by the horror in her womb. All she knew was the endless carnage she had to endure. She may have been there months, but if felt more like years.

She thought often of Stanley and how they'd parted. She wondered about the lengths to which he'd gone to find her. Had he been as out of his mind as Peter? Rose wondered if Peter would have been so desperate to find Bethany if he'd known where it would lead him?

She scratched at her leg. The blood coating her thighs was dried and flaking, making her raw skin itch. Pints and pints of it had poured out of her this time. The sheets and mattress had absorbed it all. Drank it down until there was hardly a faded stain left. The bed always devoured it. Rose had come to believe that was how it fed.

There was often cartilage or shreds of torn flesh in the blood. One time Rose saw an eyeball, with the optic nerve still attached. She had screamed then, and beaten her fists against the distended skin of her huge stomach. But it did no good. It didn't stop him. Nothing could stop him.

Once the blood had been fully absorbed by the bed, the whole process generally started again. Knowing what was going to happen next didn't make it any easier on Rose. She gripped the bed sheets and ground her teeth. The muscles in her calves knotted as her toes curled into her feet. She'd come to hate the waiting worse than all the other indignities she had to suffer.

The child within her wanted to be fed and a true mother will do anything, go to any lengths, to take care of her child. Rose's child did not draw sustenance from an umbilical cord, nor from her dry and sagging breasts. Her unborn wanted vengeance, to suckle at the teat of the aeternae ultionis.

Rose neither ate nor drank any more. Whatever was in her womb was doing that for both of them. Though her term was long overdue he refused to leave her. Her body was his to do with as he pleased now. His hideous appetites kept her alive, even though she did not share them.

The flesh along Rose's stomach began to ripple, a violent tremor made its way across the whole of her midriff. This was how it usually started. Rose felt, once again, the immense internal pressure that came with the process.

The skin around her midsection began to stretch and grow out of all proportion, as something pushed its way up from inside her. Rose groaned and screamed. An outline of shoulders, and the back of an adult head, could be clearly seen beneath the skin. Where it came from, how it appeared and grew so quickly, Rose had no idea. All she knew was the sudden, unbearable pain as her womb expanded well past its breaking point.

Her intestines and other internal organs shifted to accommodate the immense new bulk with an agony that was beyond Rose's power to express. She simply had to bear it. To endure the intrusion of this fully grown human form where it had no natural right to be.

Sometimes she could tell whether it was Peter or Bethany. She could catch a stray thought and identify it, in the same way she perceived her unborn child's brooding mind. Usually she was only aware of their terror.

Terror, and the dawning realisation that they were trapped inside an impossibly small space, a space that should be the beginning of life, but was now the site of endless, endless death.

Trapped with a tiny, vicious creature they had wronged, to whom they had promised life but brought only death and double cross.

A tiny, vicious creature with impossibly sharp teeth and claws and an insatiable need to be redressed.

Their screams and pleas did them no good. The contract was watertight, they were lawyers, they should have known. There was no escape, they were to be punished over and over and over again.

Stanley had been right. Rose's womb was an instrument of revenge. The emptiness that filled Rose made it so easy for people to get inside her. And when they did, something deep within her always died.

in search of silver boughs

Hers is a girthless restraint, thorns at her ribs… stones in her heart.

Ishtabelle bows to her mother, allowing the older woman's stroking fingers to tangle themselves in her billowing hair before the sad goodbye rips them apart.

Clouds peel from a gutless moon as the child traipses through the snow, bathing in a cruel light. Her tears freeze on her cheeks and she wonders for the thousandth time if she can do it, if she can release her mother from the hell into which she is bound. Ishtabelle wraps herself in a cloak of fur; it is as thick as a bear's but clings to her skin as thin as a spider's web and is half as warm. Below her feet the white earth trembles bringing her to a weary halt.

"My lady," Ishtabelle casts her gaze to the skies, to the lunar spectre glowing through winter's mist. "I am lost. If you can only guide me I will repay you with my very soul."

~

Boots. Boots. Boots... and not a pair to suit. They didn't make them like they used to. Emmeline picked up a clumpy, calf-length pair in a sickly tan colour; she held them by the tips of her thumb and forefinger, a sneer dragging at her mouth. An assistant spotted his customer's distaste and plucked them from her hand before she could throw them across the shop.

"May I assist?" he asked, a twist at his hips and a flicking gaze that summed his customer up in a moment. "Something for the more mature woman, perhaps. A flatter heel, a wider fit?" His chin trembled at his own importance, and he regretted his sour wit in an instant.

She had him by the throat.

She had him by the hips.

She let him simmer in his own reality. He quickly came to the boil.

Emmeline allowed him to slip to her very slim, very fine feet – clad, he realised as his slack mouth hit them, in red snakeskin stilettos. He had no time to regret his words before the woman stepped away, leaving his soul with a heart-shaped hole packed-to-overflowing with regret. He had just enough time to contemplate misbegotten hope before he died.

Paris oozed with damp. Autumn's rain had left the city sodden. Slum-house walls and majestic mausoleum-styled buildings glistened with dull perspiration. Rats spewed from badly-maintained drains, some dead and fit to rot, others streaming away from unwelcome daylight. Emmeline kicked a pair of rodents that were simultaneously eating and fornicating in the gutter. They squealed beneath her heavy blow and scampered off in separate directions, unsated. *Think your damned selves lucky*, the woman thought. Her days of love were over; a glimmer of hot desire occasionally sparked deep within her soul, filling her with regret – but it would disperse as soon as it began. A squib as damp as Paris.

She wandered for hours through tight streets, through wide open squares packed with angry traffic and in and out of an array of parks. The trees were long-empty of leaves; even the evergreens lacked lustre. She stopped beneath a yew, its ancient branches held aloft with ornate Victorian scaffolding, and approached its flaky trunk. Whenever Emmeline came here the memories flooded back, teasing... unclear. They called of purpose, of longing and Emmeline fought to recall what she was looking for. She stroked the tree bark.

"Let me see it. Tell me the story." She breathed in the noxious air beneath the boughs, allowing the hallucinations to come, and like a shaman drifting naked and effortlessly through snow, she allowed herself to rise up, up, up...

Wild winds licked at her hair, at her neck in an eager caress. Freezing whispers stabbed at Emmeline's cheeks as the temperature dropped in waves until her breath formed clouds of crumbling ice that sprinkled from her lips. She sucked it in, blew it out – and knew she had to go to England. For that, she would need those boots.

Frost patches speckled the ground like mould blooms. Blades of grass stood stiff, edged with crisp, sparkling prisms. Emmeline trod over them, trying to avoid breaking their splendour, but walking in stiletto heels is an art at the best of times and she uttered a silent prayer on behalf of her ankles. It was no good; the shops of the rue du Faubourg Saint-Honoré couldn't cater for her explicit requirements so she had no choice but to return to *him*, Fugueur, cobbler to the underworld – and she hated him.

With a sigh loud enough to startle a gathering of tiny birds from their red berry feast, Emmeline headed toward the park gate. Lovers young and old embraced on benches along the path, some holding hands and smiling, others getting close to needing a room. All of them ignored the lithe woman wrapped in mulberry silk, a shawl of fine ebony mohair draped across her shoulders, but each man and every woman shivered inwardly and hugged their partner closer as she passed them by. Later, their dreams would speak of loss and mourning, and they would awaken with the sensation of having forgotten something so important that they might die if they couldn't recall it.

Fugueur's den sat behind an eighteenth century shop front. Its curved window frames, painted in carmine red, still held the original glass; the bespoke shutters clung to the crumbling walls and had seen better days but they had been that way since Emmeline last came there, temporarily destitute and with holes in her cat skin slippers. The display hadn't changed; babies' booties, gentlemen's Brogues and ladies' sensible sandals, all covered in a light film of dust. A row of lasts in varying shapes and sizes hung from a rusting metal rack – they were mostly for show; hers – an exact replica of her feet – would be in the back, in their box, just waiting. She approached the shop, seeing even at a distance that a card hung in the door at a wonky angle with *Fermé* painted on it in an archaic font. Closed. By the time she reached the cracked pavement the sign said *Ouvert*. Just like always.

A bell jangled as she pushed the door open. The shop appeared empty but she could smell the eternal odour of meat broth and leather polish; it rushed into her nose and settled at the back of her tongue.

"Fugueur?" she called.

From somewhere within the shop came a dull scraping sound; a stool being pushed back. Slow, heavy footsteps came toward her and she stood tall, her jaw jutting, lips tight.

"Ma petite Emmeline."

The cobbler filled the doorway, blocking the light. A giant of a man. He cocked his head on one side and gave her an ugly wink.

"I know," she said. "You've been waiting for me."

Fugueur laughed, a sharp, barking grunt.

"You flatter yourself. I have many clients other than you." He drew his fingers to his lips and started to chew on a shoelace. "What do you need?"

His gaze rested on the stilettos and he smirked.

"Boots," Emmeline replied. "I need boots – again."

Fugueur frowned.

"What did you do with the last pair? They should have lasted a lifetime, even *your* lifetime."

Memories played in Emmeline's head, taunting her with their vagueness.

"I... I'm not sure. I think they were stolen – I can't remember." She looked away from the cobbler whose expression had turned. A vein pulsed in his mighty forehead.

"Stolen? What do you think you were doing? Anyone wearing my shoes will walk forever, you know that."

Rare tears threatened to rise but Emmeline gulped them back.

"No doubt whoever took them had no idea; there's probably some old tramp wandering the world wishing he could just rip them off his feet and die in peace. At least he'd remember who he was, where he'd come from."

Unlike me.

Fugueur watched in silence, then nodded.

"You know the price." A statement, not a question.

"Yes."

"Then let's make you comfortable."

~

It wasn't having to share the cobbler's bed that nauseated her the most, although that was bad enough, it was the giving up of hair – even a few strands; the release of fluids, the pairing of toenails, the peeling of skin. Every day for a week whilst he created the most perfect and well-fitting boots any living person could desire, Emmeline gave parts of herself to him. In all that time, he never asked where she was going, but he knew her destination, of that much Emmeline was sure.

"You can leave tomorrow; they're almost ready."

Desperate for this moment to come and go so that she could continue her search Emmeline let Fugueur have his clumsy way one last time, and prepared for the final payment.

"Where's best?" she asked, turning her hands over to expose her wrists.

Fugueur looked up from his hammering and shook his head.

"No, that would release too much; I just need a few drops – one for the right boot, one for the left." He tapped his chest. "And one to keep here – just in case." He picked up a shiny steel pin and stuck it quickly into the pad of Emmeline's thumb. She gasped at the pain such a small weapon could make. The cobbler squeezed and bent over her hand to lick off the first drop of blood then turned to the soft leather insert of the left boot, and spat the blood onto its base. He quickly slid the insert into the boot and repeated the action for the other one. "Now it's my turn."

Fugueur drew Emmeline's thumb slowly into his mouth and began to suck, his eyes closed. Gradually the hand turned blue, and cold... throbbing.

"I think that's all I have to give," Emmeline said, her voice sounding faraway. She felt Fugueur wrap his tongue around her thumb and he gulped hard before releasing her. When he opened his eyes they were black with ecstasy.

"Then that is all I need," he slurred, drunk with the taste of her. Emmeline knew from experience that whenever the cobbler thought of her from now on her hand would freeze – but not as much as her soul – and that he'd know where she was, some small respite should she need rescuing.

She spent the following morning packing a small holdall; Fugueur watched her as she dressed and before passing her new boots over he dropped something onto her lap.

Emmeline stared up at the giant and was bemused to find him wearing a coy expression.

"For me?"

Fugueur shrugged.

The small gift had been wrapped in maroon tissue paper, tied about with a delicately knotted silver ribbon. Emmeline pulled the bow gently apart; inside lay the thinnest material she had ever seen. She pulled it out to reveal two matching pieces.

"Silk stockings?"

"Spider silk. They'll keep you warm, and will never tear. I thought you might like to wear them under your boots when you go to England."

He *did* know.

"Thank you," she said. And meant it.

She left at noon. Paris was no longer dirty with damp but blinding with light snowfall. Fugueur refused to come to the door but gave her cheek a wet kiss before turning his back and heading down to the cellar. As she stepped over the threshold onto the pavement the cobbler's voice rang up the stairs.

"I hope you find her."

She closed the door, the bell jangling a sullen goodbye. The card already said *Fermé*.

"Thank you," Emmeline whispered. *I hope I find her too. If only I knew who she was.*

~

The yew bled with berries that had sprung from its

branches in the weeks she'd been gone. They blazed bright in the mixed hues of browns and evergreens studding the park, offering nourishment, knowledge... and danger. Theirs was a poison she must risk. The promise of death, the spark to save a life long-yearned for. Emmeline gathered a small handful and pressed them into her mouth to suck. Unlike the clever birds that spat or shat the deathly seeds from the fruit, Emmeline consumed the entire berry – and despite her immortality, lay down to await the consequences of human suffering.

Pain was something Emmeline had become oblivious to over the centuries – and she was more used to meting it out than receiving it – but the agony coursing through her gut as the black seeds did their vicious best to void her of life was excruciating. She could not have screamed for help if she'd wanted to with a fat tongue choking her throat, and while Emmeline – once so regal – spasmed in and out of consciousness, Parisians passed her by in distaste, just another addict to spoil the beauty of an otherwise perfect day. Gradually the convulsions began to ebb. Emmeline stared around at the filth emitted from her own body and crawled away from it. A disfunctioning fountain stood a few yards south, its verdigris dolphin's head crying out empty words over a small pond. The ice Emmeline found there broke easily. She stripped herself of everything but her boots and ran a sharp shard over her skin from the top of her head to the base of her kneecaps. Tendrils of algae dripped in slimy caress as their winter captor melted from the heat of the woman's body. The cold and the greenery between them cleansed deeper than the reluctant pores and she felt her soul lift with new clarity. She lifted her soiled clothes and threw them into the air where they twisted in a sudden cyclone. As they fell back to the earth a small crowd gathered causing the park-keeper to investigate the spectacle and come hurrying at her across the grass. Emmeline reached up and grabbed the garments fluttering towards her as the man began to shout and blow an old-fashioned whistle. She held out long arms as a corset of silver taffeta wrapped itself around her, squeezing her waist and plumping her breasts as leather ribbons tied themselves at her back. Looking down she found her thighs already clad in Fugueur's spider-silk stockings, but they were not visible for long, as a lilac grey dress grew over her body, its soft jersey cotton tight and warm against her arms, layers of sheerest tatters floating in the breeze. Emmeline felt the weight of heavy brocade on her shoulders and welcomed her old cloak, which looked as if the last embroidery stitch had been sewn only the day before.

"She looks like a princess," a little boy beamed up at her, his voice clear through the bemused chatter of the crowd.

Emmeline found herself smiling, a sensation long-forgotten.

"And this one became queen," she said, sending a chill through people's hearts and tears into the boy's eyes.

A shrill whistle pierced the air.

"Hey, what do you think you're..."

Emmeline didn't hear the collective gasp as she vanished from Paris in a sudden storm of snow.

~

It had been so long, the concept of 'home' meant nothing; once she'd been released from the tree all memory of her origins had been swept away with a besom blast. All she'd been left with was the yearning, and the magic. And now the memories were returning, layer upon layer of feelings, of recollections. *This* was home, and this was where she would find her daughter, her only child.

Emmeline arrived in England in the middle of a frosted fallow field, almost blinded by a low sun. With nothing to identify the place or the time she could only assume she hadn't slipped back to another century, and marched instinctively north until the sounds of urban life began to filter through. The whoosh of cars on a distant road, a train chugging slowly nearby, and above, distorted trails of cloud that could only have been deposited there by escaping planes. She found the railway bank and stuck as close to it as she could without severing skin on brambles until she spotted a tiny station, brick-built with empty platforms. The woodland and hedgerow beneath her feet gave way to a small path that led over a bridge and down to a platform where the waiting rooms were closed and the ticket office empty. Emmeline laughed out loud; she wasn't even sure where she wanted to go, but a faded map and a crumpled timetable hanging from a pale green wall gave her the chance to study her options. It seemed she was at Balcombe, a Sussex station through which trains ran regularly but didn't always stop. She traced a finger along a line until it reached London, and that was that. London was where she'd find her.

"Ishtabelle," she uttered her daughter's name for the first time in six hundred years.

Had a train not come racing into the station at that very moment Emmeline would have collapsed in a sea of tears.

~

Money was of no concern. The cloak carried it in abundance, though it eventually faded to plain paper in any recipient's hand, the illusion lost. Emmeline bought a ticket from a grumpy conductor who told her she'd need to alight at London Bridge station. He stared at the strange woman long after she occupied her seat. There was something cold about her, and as he prepared to end his shift he vowed to wrap his long-suffering wife in a heavy embrace when he arrived home, and that he would never stray again.

Paris was a vibrant, bustling city but nothing as loud as London. Emmeline felt herself drawn to the Thames as the train alternately crossed it and ran alongside it. The answer was here, deep in its tidal waters. But not yet. First she had to find *him*.

In the midst of the rushing fleet of passengers Emmeline stood still to get her bearings. The tunnel amplified sounds of feet, of voices shouting into phones or from stalls selling wares; it distorted her instincts so she ran for the nearest exit to get her back into the fresh but grubby air. Once outside she took the deepest breath. *Concentrate. Find her.* She closed her eyes and quite clearly saw a famous painting; everyone knew it, it was one of the Pre-Raphaelite classics. Emmeline had always loved this particular work because of its theme, and its extraordinary beauty, but now...

Without wishing to bring attention to herself Emmeline joined the queue for a cab rather than jumping into the first one that arrived, as was her habit. As it was, she didn't have to wait long.

"Where to, love?" the driver spoke into a microphone from behind his screen.

"I want to see Ophelia."

Such is the knowledge of the London cabbie that he knew exactly what his passenger meant.

"Tate Britain," he said, and left her to watch the city as he sped through the streets. Later, he forgot the woman that had tipped him heavily and it was the barman that threw his maudlin customer out who found himself with a till full of blank paper.

"I'm here to see Ophelia," Emmeline announced in a clear voice but in an accent the Gallery receptionist found hard to place.

"Millais's Ophelia? It's part of a special exhibition at the moment, with related works by Millais as well as paintings and drawings by other artists, both contemporary and modern." She pointed at a small poster on the desk that declared the cost of entry and the programme price. "Would you..."

"Yes," Emmeline said, pulling what appeared to be a twenty pound note from her cloak. "I'd like a ticket and a programme."

The exhibition gallery was surprisingly empty. People from different walks of life and descent wandered back and forth to peer at the works on show. A handful of art students occupied seats and benches making copies and pastiches of the great painting, one young man kept glancing up to see if anyone was observing him instead of the paintings. He would live a life of perpetual disappointment, Emmeline foresaw. She travelled the room, spending time at each piece but feeling her hair prickle as she drew closer to the object she'd come looking for. Her cloak stroked the vain student's knees as she passed and she was satisfied to hear him shudder in short ecstasy. He was quickly forgotten as she reached the corner of the room. There, barely six inches wide by five inches high in a thick and ornate gilded frame - a painting, not much more than a sketch - portraying the face of Ishtabelle.

"Beautiful, isn't she?"

The voice at her shoulder pierced Emmeline's daydream and she turned to look the curator in the eye. A thin, middle-aged woman with a Chanel haircut and suit, but without the allure, gave an alarming smile and gazed once again at the painting. Emmeline opened her mouth to speak but the curator wanted the opportunity to display her knowledge.

"This is our little mystery," she said. "It was found in Millais's studio with other pieces by his students but it is a different style, some have even suggested it is older than Millais's own Ophelia and is what inspired him to paint her with her hands splayed out to the side, the flowers dying in her right hand."

Emmeline nodded. "It *is* older."

"Well," the curator frowned, "we can't say for sure. The materials used are certainly of a greater age but they could have been acquired by an antiquary specialist. There's a signature on the back – Augustus Flinch. But we have no record of this artist so..."

Emmeline leaned forward to touch the painting. The curator grabbed her hand but released it as a shot of pain coursed through her fingers.

"Madam. You can't touch..."

"Woman. This painting is of my daughter, and Augustus Flinch? He was... *is* her father. This picture belongs to me."

She snapped her fingers. Every person, every visitor, student and member of staff in the building closed their eyes and fell into a momentary stupor. When they awoke, wondering how such a hangover could have occurred, the Flinch painting was gone without a single alarm having sounded to shrill the ears.

"I'll find you Flinch," Emmeline swore as she ran through the streets of London. "And you'll give me my daughter back."

She clung to the centuries-old painting, her intuition dragging her towards Chelsea. Even in her determined walk to reach Flinch she wondered how the gallery could have missed the obvious; Ishtabelle – the subject of the sketch – was not drowning in the water like the tragic Ophelia; she was *under* the water, under the ice – staring up and calling for her mother. And she was very much alive.

~

The smell of him, the very essence of his being, hit Emmeline as she neared his house. Her legs ached with the exercise but Fugueur's boots carried her on. Flinch had cast heavy protection around the property, which stood halfway down St. Luke's Street off the King's Road and occupied a corner plot overlooking railed gardens. The colours hummed in Emmeline's vision, spiking and sparking with warning heat. She stood for a moment to catch her breath and watched how people crossed the road rather than walk directly past the three-storey townhouse; the pulsing vibrations were not visible to the common man but his instincts troubled him enough to keep away. Emmeline's feet tapped the pavement, ready to move her on, so she submitted, observing the house intently until she stood opposite, unfazed by the protective barrier but overwhelmed by Flinch's scent. He came from a deeper forest than she, one shrouded by shadow with trees half-buried in mulch. The smell of pine resin and thriving rot had been her first experience of him, and one she should not have perpetuated. But lovers with badness in their blood are the most addictive – and when Emmeline was a young queen Augustus Flinch turned her head in the way only the dangerous can.

A man's figure moved against a window on the top floor. He lingered, staring down at Emmeline, but the soft light behind him disguised his features. It mattered not; Emmeline crossed the road and although the air crackled as she mounted the black-and-white-tiled steps, she knew that her daughter's father was home.

She picked up the weighty brass knocker and let it fall heavily. Then she knocked again... once, twice. The black door opened slowly.

"Come in," was all he said.

~

The Chelsea house had been exquisitely renovated and still retained its original features. When Emmeline stepped over the threshold it resonated with the souls of those that had lived there over two hundred years earlier, when the entire terrace had been a slum of dwelling houses with labourers and laundresses and Thames-men and filthy children all living and dying together, ten or more to a single room. Her senses told her that the area had changed in the 1980s and now these properties were for millionaires and investors, a new breed of scum.

"I see you landed on your feet," she said, declining to "*take a seat*" in a worn Chesterfield.

"I do well enough," Flinch replied. "It's a temporary residence."

"I bet it is. Still in the soul-ripping business? Got somewhere to move onto once you've sucked the vulnerable dry around here?"

Flinch grinned and even then Emmeline felt her gut stir. She swore under her breath. He hadn't changed – the blackest of hair, the blackest of eyes, the blackest of hearts – he was delicious. But she would not fall for him again. Not after everything.

"Oh, I think you'd find me quite the normal artist these days," he said, swinging a hand around to indicate the paintings adorning his wall. "It suits me better, don't you think? Less messy. Attracts a better clientele than the murdering, abducting type."

Despite herself Emmeline scanned the walls. The paintings were extraordinary, and similar in style not only to the sketch she clutched in her hand but to something far more familiar that nagged at her brain. She approached a rendition of three naked women entwined around an oak; pulpous and fleshy, their limbs appeared to sink in and out of one another with no feet and no hands visible. Each female stared up into the leaves in wanton desire. Emmeline shuddered as Augustus traced a finger across the back of her neck and tugged on a wisp of hair.

"Maiden, mother, crone – do you like them? They remind me of you – all of them."

Not deigning to answer Emmeline looked to the edges of the canvas in search of a signature. When she found it, it was all she could do not to gasp.

"Trigwell? *You're* Goethe Trigwell?"

Flinch took an ostentatious bow.

"I'm flattered you've heard of me, of my work."

Anger fizzed into Emmeline's throat and burst from her mouth in a spray of expletives.

"Heard of you? You're all over my fucking walls!"

She threw herself at him, forgetting to use her magic and he grabbed her wrists, pulling her towards him until their breath mingled.

"Ah yes. Your bijou palace in Paris, a crumbling pile within sniffing distance of the Seine."

Emmeline pushed him away.

"How do you know that? I didn't even know who you were. Shit, I didn't even know who *I* was."

Finch's smile faded.

"I know everything about you since you escaped the tree, Emmeline. I know what you did to Ishtabelle."

Emmeline fell silent. She had no idea what he was talking about. "Come with me," he said, yanking her wrist.

"Ouch. Stop – you don't have to hurt me – I'll follow."

"No. You first – up the stairs. It's in the room on the top floor."

The warmth of her ex-lover at her back comforted her, a twist of emotions that spiralled through her fear to curdle as love and hate. Would Ishtabelle be waiting at the top of the stairs? The floorboards creaked as she stepped on them and Emmeline briefly wondered if Flinch had bought the effect to order, everything in the house seemed 'just so'.

"Nice boots," Flinch uttered. She chose not to respond, sure he also knew everything about Fugueur and how she'd had to pay for the footwear.

The top step loomed closer. It seemed higher than the others, more of a shelf. Emmeline pulled herself up by the balustrade and had to duck to avoid hitting her head on the slant-eaved ceiling. The combination of the long staircase and mis-matched floor-to-ceiling space struck her as odd.

"To the left. It's the only room up here."

There was no carpet to soften her steps as she made her way down a short corridor which led onto an open room with no door. At first glance the room appeared empty, its windows bare of curtains, no furniture save a simple hardback chair in the corner. A metal box clicked and whirred on the opposite side of the room, attached to the wall just below the ceiling. Emmeline made to enter the room but once again Flinch caught her wrist.

"Augustus. I keep telling you; I'm not running away."

He ignored her.

"Look down. This is what you came to see."

The floor, that she had assumed covered with a pale grey linoleum, twinkled with frosted light; ice. Emmeline turned to face Flinch but he stared past her at the frozen floor of water that almost filled the width and breadth of the room.

"Go in, carefully. You can edge your way round without slipping."

For once Emmeline did as she was told. Flinch remained at the doorway.

"Sit down," he instructed.

Emmeline lowered herself onto the chair, the tatters of her silk jersey dress fluttering gently down around her. She dared to look toward the ice and saw her there, gazing from the frozen bed – outwards, upwards, directly at her.

"Ishtabelle."

The water cracked.

Ishtabelle's roaring gasp shook the entire house as the ice melted around her. Outside, the day turned to filth with storm clouds quickly gathering to evacuate a vertical sheet of hail and rain. Londoners ran to shelter in doorways rubbing their faces where the crystalline downpour had sliced at their skin. Sirens wailed. Babies wailed. And inside Augustus Flinch's house Emmeline wailed with the ferocity of blind regret.

When she finally looked up from her keening spasm of tears her daughter stood before her, a teenager – older than when she had last seen her so, so long ago. White-gold hair hung almost to the floor, curling as it dried. Her pale blue eyes were wide – huge. Emmeline wiped away a stab of jealousy as Augustus approached the girl with a soft robe in his arms; he laid it gently over her shoulders and helped her arms into the sleeves before tying the robe around her waist. Ishtabelle glanced down at her mother's hand.

"You found the key."

Her words came in a breathy whisper. Emmeline looked from the girl to the painting, and back again.

"Yes," she said. "Your father, he…"

"Painted me. He didn't want to. He didn't want you anywhere near me after what you did, the lies you told. But I made him do it." Emmeline held her arms out to her daughter but the girl stepped back. "Don't you ever touch me again."

Flinch had returned to the edge of the room; he watched them from the doorway, saying nothing. Emmeline struggled to remember but it was still all so patchy; made queen at sixteen after her parents died of a fleeting plague, meeting Flinch, falling pregnant… Banishment, yes – they were banished across the sea to wander the cold lands where nights were long and daylight came briefly. She shook her head, confused.

"What are you thinking, Emmeline. Tell us."

Flinch remained at the door but he seemed closer, as though he had boomed the instruction directly into Emmeline's ear. She repeated her thoughts; both Flinch and Ishtabelle shook their heads sadly, and she faltered.

"Am I wrong?" She stared at her daughter.

"Go on, mother. Tell it as you see it, as you remember it."

Emmeline felt like a child again, admonished at every step. She drew her arms around herself in defence.

"Well, we travelled the forests together – living with the deer, and the bears and the wolves, trading our magic with the people we found so that we could survive."

"So that *you* could survive," Flinch corrected. Emmeline frowned and continued. "And then... and then, your father and I had a disagreement and oh! Ishtabelle, he tried to kill me – right there and then – so I knocked him down and I took you, my love, as far as my feet could carry us and we were fine for a while until," she stood up suddenly and pointed at Flinch. "Until you tricked me into meeting you then wove your wicked magic to trap me inside the silver birch before disappearing like the coward you are."

"Coward?"

"Yes. What about your daughter? What about Ishtabelle? How was she supposed to survive without me?"

The floor creaked as Flinch stepped into the room. "Emmeline, I did it for Ishtabelle's sake. I was coming back for her but by the time I returned you'd sent her into the wilderness to sell her soul to the Goddess, just so you could return and start killing again."

"What? What are you talking about? Killing who?"

Flinch took a deep breath. "Your parents for a start – that is, after you'd disposed of your sisters and your brother."

Memories rushed in, swirled and left again.

"No," Emmeline said. "They all died together – there was a plague. And I was the last one left to take the throne. I had responsibilities." She wandered in a ramble of words. "I suppose I was just too young to deal with that. Augustus, I..."

"No. You poisoned your entire family." He waved a hand over Emmeline's head, squeezing his eyes closed with a grimace. "Remember now?"

Animals, tiny creatures lured into traps then force-fed leaves and seeds and plant juices. Bigger animals, hunted and attacked with arrows, their tips coated in a sticky resin. And the children – familiar faces – Aurelia, Maude, Tomas – their sweet faces writhing and bloating as they died the most horrible deaths, the fruit in their throats removed by Emmeline's own hands as soon as they hit the ground.

Emmeline sank back onto the chair. It was like watching someone else's life-story and whilst none of it was familiar, she knew it to be true. A sheet of understanding washed over her.

"Show me."

"You're no queen, Emmeline," Flinch said, almost gently. "You had no crown. Where the hell do you think you were queen of? England was already on its fifth Henry when I met you; you were no more than a gutter-whore peddling yourself and your dirty witchcraft for money."

Emmeline felt the weight of Ishtabelle's pity on her and she looked up to see her daughter's beautiful eyes brimming with tears. "Go on," Ishtabelle said. "Show her the rest."

"Wait. But Augustus – what about my powers? Only true royal blood can wield such magic."

Flinched sighed. "It's true, you have an incredible

ability to hypnotise, persuade and create illusion, but none of it is inherited – your father, and his father before him toiled the land for little gain. Your mother came from France – the daughter of a fisherman. But somehow, somewhere in your cruel, envious child's mind you managed to tap into the ancient energies of the land and twist them to do your bidding. Magic exists already; it's around us wherever we tread, wherever we look. You are not magic yourself, Emmeline, but you are an abuser of it."

Emmeline drew herself up straight.

"And so why did you take up with me if I was so despicable?"

Ishtabelle raised her hand. "No father, I'll tell her." She approached Emmeline until there was but a foot between them. "He tried to rescue you, do you not understand? The land called to him to find you and sever your parasitic bind but you trapped him too." She looked from her mother to her father. "He fell in love with you."

Flinch turned his face away. "It's true, and it was our undoing. I was bewitched by you, you showed me secrets of the flesh, and you made me laugh with your daring. Ishtabelle made our lives perfect, a princess of nature born outside beneath the stars – do you remember that night?"

Emmeline didn't remember it at all, but when Flinch showed her she realised where that yearning, that *longing* she'd been chasing had come from. "My baby," she said. "My beautiful child."

"We lived for years in foolish happiness, making a fortune and getting ourselves in trouble for the fun of it, but when you asked me to murder for you, Emmeline, it was too much. And it was in that instant that I was reminded why I'd been sent to find you in the first place, and I realised you'd blinded me to the truth. So yes, I did lie to you. I told you we were being hunted, a price on our heads, and I took you and Ishtabelle overseas to the hidden safety of the frozen lands of the north where we wandered all those years, surviving, struggling but alive – and together."

In her mind's eye Emmeline followed the journey as Flinch described it. It felt as though it should have been blissful, just the three of them travelling wrapped in the embrace of nature but nothing, she realised, was as it seemed. Not by far. She took a deep breath and asked the question that had been creeping upward with knowing tendrils.

"What happened?"

Flinch offered her his hand, and took Ishtabelle's with the other. "Let's go downstairs, into the warmth."

~

A fire smouldered in the grate; Flinched dropped an applewood log onto the embers and prodded it into place with a poker. He poured three glasses of darkest Merlot and handed them around.

"Be careful with it, little one," he smiled at Ishtabelle. "That belly of yours has been empty for too long." His daughter took a small sip of the red wine and placed the glass on a small lacquered table. She didn't pick it up again.

"Please," Emmeline said once they were all settled in

separate armchairs. "Tell me what happened, what I did."

Flinch gave her a small nod. She had at least acknowledged an element of complicity; it was a start.

"All the time we were out in the forests, it was fine. We built temporary shelters, we hunted, we cooked. But as soon as we neared any other dwellings you... well, you *changed* Emmeline. Something inside you warped, and the larger the settlements, the villages – the worse your cravings became."

Emmeline tilted her head, experiencing none of the sensations Flinch described. "Cravings?"

Flinch hung his head then took a large gulp of wine before continuing. "You took lovers."

Emmeline suddenly found the scenario absurd. "Is that all? Augustus – from what you've shown me we shared many another's bed along the way, and I *do* remember some of those." She laughed, shaking her head, not noticing Ishtabelle look away.

"No, mother. He means you actually 'took' lovers – you watched couples make love then you killed them in their beds and fed on them."

Whether hearing such words being uttered by an innocent girl or the actual stated facts – they were enough to throw Emmeline's heart into a shudder of palpitations.

"I... I killed them?"

"Yes," Flinch said. "I didn't even know it was you the first time. I only heard about it after we'd passed through the village and the news reached the next settlement before we did. I wouldn't have thought any more about it until a year later when the same thing happened twice in succession." He stared then, deep into Emmeline's eyes, the flames from the fireplace reflecting back. "I'd already given you a lifetime of chances, Emmeline. I had no more to give you. And when I discovered you'd taken our daughter, that you'd actually taken Ishtabelle with you on a kill, then I had to stop you."

Emmeline stood up and crossed the floor to Ishtabelle's side. "Forgive me; I'm so sorry."

"Don't waste your apologies. I don't remember. Just sit down and listen."

Flinch waited until Emmeline returned to her seat before standing up. He walked back and forth in front of the fireplace, stroking his chin as he contemplated what to say next. It came.

"You see, I had to ask for help," he said.

But Emmeline *didn't* see, it wasn't clear to her at all. She waited.

"I had to go further north," Flinch went on. "I needed a bindrune, a binding... *spell* if you like."

"I know what a bindrune is Augustus, don't insult me."

"No, no – of course you're right. Well, I did go north – not far, but several days away. That's when I met your friend Fugueur, although he was called something quite different then."

Emmeline's lips tightened.

"You know the cobbler?"

"Oh, he doesn't just make and mend shoes Emmeline – as you're fully aware. His is the oldest magic of all. He works with the earth's very essence, whether it's forging anvils from mountain iron, twisting birch trees into prisons or making the most perfect pair of boots from human leather…"

"Human?"

"Of course. I don't know why you're so shocked; it was you that supplied the skin from one of your kills."

Emmeline stared down at her feet. The boots became suddenly tight, and her toes pulsed as though having the blood sucked from them. He was listening, Fugueur. And Flinch was still talking.

"He gave me what I needed, just in time, but it cost me more than a cobbler's debt, I can tell you. When I got back to where I'd left you, you were long gone. It took me six months to find you but your bloody reputation led me on. I still don't know how you managed to slaughter so many and flee before they caught you. At least I'd wrapped Ishtabelle in enough protection to keep her away from you when you went on the prowl, but it didn't stop her from knowing what you were doing. It astonishes me to this day that she loved you so much she saw past the murder. Her love alone should have been pure enough magic to stop you but you were so deeply insane, you were impenetrable."

Emmeline stared into the fireplace, the heat making her sweat. "It's like you're talking about someone else. I simply can't associate with it."

"Or acknowledge it?" Ishtabelle asked quietly.

"How can I accept something I have no recollection of? Even the glimpses you're giving me – they upset me, naturally – but that wasn't me." She sighed, a great outpouring of breath. "But had it been me, and I can see no reason why you would lie, then I am more sorry than it is possible to say. I won't deign to ask your forgiveness again, because I don't, or at least that woman – the older me – doesn't deserve it."

The three sat without speaking with only crackling wood and vague street noises to pepper the silence. Eventually Ishtabelle stood up.

"You're right. I can't forgive you. Even after Father returned and bound you inside the tree your mind was still working, scheming as always. You knew he'd go looking for me, and you tricked him into taking the wrong route so he couldn't find me. When I returned – I was gathering firewood, you probably don't remember that either – I saw what he'd done and I believed *you*. I was taken in by all your lies about him until I accepted your pleas that only *I* could save you. Me, a near-orphaned girl, alone in a wild wood. Innocent."

Emmeline hung her head. "Go on."

"We wandered, he and I for month upon month, Father looking for me, me seeking some higher magic to release you."

"But you found it," Emmeline said. "While I slept in the birch tree."

"Yes, but not where you think. I *did* offer my soul to the Goddess, like you told me – but she didn't take it, instead she led me to Father, and in turn – after he'd explained the reality of what had happened, he took me to meet Fugueur."

Emmeline's blood ran cold with the thought of how Fugueur took his payments – not her daughter, not Ishtabelle.

"You didn't…"

"Pay him?"

Flinch shook his head, joining the conversation. "No Emmeline, there was no payment, not then. Fugueur could see the purity in Ishtabelle's heart, and when she offered to sacrifice herself so that you could be released, he was obliged to accept – but with restrictions."

Emmeline reached for her daughter's hands, and this time Ishtabelle allowed her to take them. They were as sticks of frosted twigs.

"You sacrificed yourself… for me?"

Ishtabelle nodded. "Even after they told me the truth about you – because a magical sacrifice is not allowed where truth is hidden – I still wanted to save you. You were still my mother."

Years of loneliness sprung as hot tears, falling down Emmeline's face, soaking her clothes as they dripped from her chin. When she spoke, her voice juddered and she could hardly catch her breath.

"I'm so, so sorry. And so, so grateful my darling. If only I'd known, I would have searched for you. Actually, I *was* searching – I just didn't know what, or who for."

"Well that's just it Emmeline. We didn't want you to find her; we didn't want you to remember anything about her – about me, and most definitely about yourself. Fugueur kept an eye on you after you broke out of the tree – it was his magic after all, the bind was… is still there. And while you stumbled across borders, reinventing yourself before disappearing and turning up in a new town, a new city, what you *never* forgot was your own magic, and your name. So we couldn't risk you getting closer."

Emmeline shook her head, wiping her wet face with the back of her hand. "Was I ever close, Augustus?"

"Yes, often. But Fugueur had put up barricades along the entire coast of England when Ishtabelle and I returned, when our daughter insisted on being suspended within the frozen surface of the Thames until – not knowing if it would ever come to pass – your mind was healed." He swallowed a cough as his voice broke. "You wandered the low countries, down through France, Spain, Portugal and back again to Paris, always to Paris where Fugueur had based himself. Do you recall the first time you met him? He wanted you to keep that memory."

A wintery, showery day, Emmeline recalled, as sharply as if it had happened yesterday. She caught her throat with a trembling hand as a vision tumbled at speed through her mind. She had taken rooms in a large house, otherwise unoccupied, as was her wont, with only a housekeeper, maid and carriage driver from the same family as staff. They lived in a small cottage at the edge of the property; far enough away not to be seen but close enough should Emmeline need them. That day she had demanded the carriage take her into the city. The driver had been astonished to see his mistress dressed as a man, though he saw far worse over the years.

Emmeline wandered the dirty streets, not really knowing what she was looking for. She picked at wares but turned her nose up at everything until she reached a long arched wall with blacksmiths, basket makers and there... at the end, a cobbler. Her feet couldn't take her to him fast enough. The huge man grunted at her. He turned his back as she approached.

"Is my custom not good enough for you?" Emmeline said.

"My work is too fine for one such as you," the cobbler retorted, then spat on the floor.

Emmeline was furious, and curious. She was unaccustomed to being denied but equally knew she needed this man, actually *needed* him. "Sir," she said. "I require a collection of boots and shoes."

"Then you can look elsewhere. I have more work than I can deal with without your custom."

Urgency surged into Emmeline's very core. She *had* to have footwear created by this great oaf of a man; it was as though her life depended on it.

"I can pay well."

"You don't know my price," the cobbler said quietly. He turned then to face her. "Money does not buy my boots, Queen Emmeline."

And so it had started; two months of bootmaking, of trying on leather and velvet slippers, of succumbing to Fugueur's great bulk in his bed – or where the opportunity struck – and releasing parts of herself to create the bond. The footwear lasted a near-eternity and it was only as it reached final disrepair, or indeed was stolen, that Emmeline found herself thinking about Fugueur and needing to seek him out. She never questioned his magic, she only knew that for as long as *she* had lived and roamed, he had lived longer.

"He had you in his grasp," Flinch spoke, breaking Emmeline's sinister reverie. "He has you still."

Emmeline nodded. It all made some kind of peculiar sense, though she was not sure she understood it. She looked up at the father of her child.

"And you? Augustus Flinch, Goethe Trigwell...?"

Flinch smiled and Emmeline remembered why the girl she'd once been had fallen in love with this charming man; it wasn't the danger after all, it was the truth behind those black eyes – they weren't a mirror, they were a pool. And he hadn't led her into a life of depravity and lack of care; it was *she* that had corrupted him.

"Despite what you think," he said. "I never left you, not really. The jewels at your throat? I'm in every stone. The silk on your skin? I can read it like a book. And my paintings – not just Trigwell's, though I confess I have enjoyed his success most of all – but the miniatures you carry with you, the great portraits in the style of Gainsborough that hang in your dusty hallways... I painted many of them, just for you. Louis, Gustave, Marie, Charles... I see through their eyes. I've been watching you Emmeline, waiting for the madness to end."

In the great fireplace the flames grew tall, throwing willowy ochre shadows across the walls, across the faces of the room's occupants. Emmeline stood once more and crossed to the hearth, her back to Augustus and Ishtabelle.

"And has it ended? This madness you speak of?"

She quivered as Flinch approached her from behind. His scent was overpowering now, like all the earth's richest glories secreting from his skin in a golden, drifting hue. He kissed the back of her neck.

Emmeline's boots moved against her shins. She didn't need to look down to know the laces were unravelling, Fugueur's fingers undoing the binds. Air blew cool against her face. It grew in swirling wafts around the room coursing through everyone's hair, lifting the heavy fabric at the windows and rattling frames against the walls. The tinkling of a thousand glass bells grew in Emmeline's ears until the ringing became a torrent of chimes and they shattered; every sound of every shard a memory – envy, murder, hatred. The sensations stabbed her and she spun around to face the people that throughout her long, long life had given everything to save her; even an echo of Fugueur danced large beside them, a mallet in one hand, a ribbon in the other. They all stared in silence, waiting... until it came.

Guilt.

Pulsating, debilitating spasms of guilt.

Emmeline dropped to her knees and the roaring wind died. The bell-shards, visible now, fell all around her in a crystal rain. As they melted in the heat of the fire so did the pain, ebbing slowly to leave the memories entwined within a web of resolve to right the wrongs of the past.

Ishtabelle came to her mother's frail side and helped her to her feet; they were bare.

"I think you have your answer," she said. "I think the madness has gone."

~

The Thames froze again by the end of that winter. Emmeline would have loved to have skated upon it but didn't think the time was right, would *ever* be right to ask Ishtabelle to walk on water after spending so long beneath it. She hugged her daughter close, the pair of them curled up on a soft, new sofa in Flinch's living-room.

"Mother? Do you think he'll come back?"

Emmeline took her time before replying.

"I don't know my darling. I kept him on the earth, *above* the earth against his will for far too long. He is of older blood, you know that. He has more people to save and guide onto the right paths. He might come back, but it could take forever and a day." She glanced towards the window, the lights of Chelsea flickering through the glass, distorted by the falling snow. "Or it could just take a moment."

Ishtabelle nodded, still a young girl despite her immense age. "I miss him."

Emmeline kissed the top of her daughter's head, and stroked a wave of hair from her face. She missed Augustus too, and she missed Ishtabelle even though she was sitting right next to her. This was what love meant; if only she'd known before.

~

Outside, the man people knew as Augustus Flinch spoke ancient words into his hands and blew them over his house. His girls would be safe there until he returned someday. A chill breeze ran through his black hair like prying fingers and he turned his face up to the moon.

"Thank you," he said, and her light shone upon him. He had sold his soul to the Goddess once upon a time. It was time to buy it back.

once and ever after

Once upon a time we lived happily ever after. Or so we are told.

So we are told by a soothing and trusted voice as we close our eyes to sleep, impressionable and drifting away to construct our dreams. We are told again and again as the pages of the book of bedtime stories turn an ancient gold and the creases in the spine that mark our favourites become deeper and deeper. These stories are within us all, and despite their ugly sisters, trolls under bridges and wicked stepmothers, what we most remember are the handsome princes and beautiful princesses, the gold at the end of the rainbow and the happy ever after endings.

Is that why we are so confused, so unprepared when our lives, our stories, are so depressingly straight: grimly predictable parallel lines running alongside each other with a monotonous nine-till-five rhythm? We stumble through our worlds of congestion and pollution, of petty crime and job insecurity, of sex scandals and soap gossip, and all the while the evil trolls sit in their palaces and run their multi-national business conglomerates, and the beautiful princesses hover around and wait to be included in their wills. Our handsome princes lose their crowns of hair and cultivate beer bellies. Our pots of gold, if they are found at all, are eaten away by insurances fees, pension contributions, and sleight of hand taxes. And as for happy ever after endings...

The adult in us knows life is like this: dirty and unfair. But the sleeping child within still hopes that one day something will change, the glass slipper will fit *our* foot, and our story will break away in a new magical direction. But it never seems to happen and we sigh as we wake from our dreams, trying not to think too hard about the story we read to our children the previous night.

But there must be some lifelines that break away from the flock, some radical swerves in direction that save the magic in life from being caught in the drizzle and washed down the gutter? Happiness ever after may be impossible but can't those of us who are deserving have a decent share of happiness, and so let the tales in our heads no longer bewilder and embitter us?

Let me tell you a story – a story about two girls and a mirror that just might have been enchanted. And it starts (of course) like this:

~

Once upon a time...

...a girl called Tabatha bought a mirror. Tabatha had wanted another mirror for months, because there was a spot in her large bedroom where she liked to sit, but where she couldn't see her reflection in either of her other two mirrors. So she had wheedled and whined to her daddy, until her daddy had taken her around the fashionable London shops with his golden credit card. But all the mirrors Tabatha had seen she hadn't liked: they were all too small or too large, too circular or too angular... On the way back home Tabatha told her father how she didn't think it was fair that there wasn't a mirror in the whole of London that she liked. She told him this at some length, and her father (who had come up the hard way and had once hated girls like his daughter, until he'd married one) grunted and willed the chauffeur to hurry up and get him home away from his daughter's complaining.

His wishes didn't seem to influence the order of things much, unless they did so in an *inverse* manner. Maybe his silent prayers caused the Universe (which doesn't like being bossed around) to place the roadblock in the car's way.

Tabatha saw the cones blocking their route; behind this barrier road workers swarmed, wearing fluorescent jackets seemingly straight over their naked torsos. They didn't seem to be doing much except shouting and hacking the road to bits – it was more like a protest or nascent riot than a worksite. The blocked junction was a sort of boundary; for while the suburb on one side was spacious, tree-lined, and exclusive, the estate on the other was run down, boarded up, and dirty. The chauffeur turned down into one of its roads, saying he knew the quickest way round the obstruction. Tabatha sighed melodramatically for the benefit of her father, but she also leaned forward and looked out the car window with keen, prying eyes.

The streets gradually became curiouser and curiouser. The road between the houses was narrow and the estate seemed more overcast than where they had come from, as if suffering a harsher climate. The people outside seemed to believe this too, for they had more hunched up forms and weather beaten faces than any of Tabatha's acquaintances. Their eyes were glazed over as if not to see the dog-shit in their path or the graffiti and crudely suggestive billboards either side. Teenage girls pushed baby carriages older than they were, and the boys yelled across the street at them, then rushed impatiently past the old men laden down with off-white carrier bags.

Theirs wasn't the only car that had made this detour, and the traffic was slow moving. Tabatha saw some of the people outside look at their car with open envy; sometimes it seemed like they were looking at *her* but she knew they couldn't really see through the tinted glass windows. They couldn't see her staring. Of course, Tabatha had seen such places before, if only on a screen, but she still found it low-rent and fascinating. There were details she just couldn't understand. The old woman pulling a shopping trolley from which a Scottie dog peered for example. Couldn't the dog walk? Did these people really keep disabled pets? Such questions caught and tangled in Tabatha's thoughts. She wondered why supermarket posters made such a big deal out of 80p off a packet of cereal or 10p off a can of beans. She wondered if fish and chips really came wrapped in newspaper and if men really went into those peeling newsagents and bought pornography. She wondered what the numbers in the bookie's window *meant* and what kind of people actually bought things from a charity shop, like the one they were now passing with its sweat-soiled clothes, its dead-men suits and ten penny paperbacks, a chest of broken drawers and that awful looking mirror...

That mirror.

"Stop the car!" Tabatha shouted. Her father jerked out of the dream he had been having in the back-seat.

"There's nowhere to park," he said, but by then Tabatha had already been impatiently instructing the chauffeur to stop in a spot quite clearly marked *Buses Only*. The chauffeur, happy to abdicate responsibility for a decision that might annoy his boss, smoothly did so, then turned off the engine and sat back with his hands off the wheel.

Tabatha dashed from the car, ignoring whatever her father was saying, and back up the street towards the charity shop. The beating insistence that she *had* to have that mirror allowed her to block out the oddness of what she doing; she was running, which she never did, and so the street was blurred in her vision, like looking through cheap glass. The pedestrians in her way seemed too tall and she dodged around them without seeing them clearly.

She burst into the charity shop, accompanied by a weak-willed trill from the bell as she opened the door. She paused on the threshold, uncertain as she never would have been in a fashionable boutique or salon. Was she really about to do this; was she really here?

"Shut the door love it's bloody freezing," someone said, but she couldn't see where in the shop the masculine voice had come from.

Cautiously, but still feeling the excitement beat through her, Tabatha moved over to the window display to where the mirror was. She felt that everyone in the shop was looking at her, the women glancing at her obliquely from beneath headscarves or wind-harried hairdos, the men eying her up directly, their faces all dryness lines and stubble.

No one came to help her, and she didn't want to delay, so Tabatha picked up the heavy mirror and struggled with it to the cash desk. She tried to avoid making eye contact with anyone, and consequently bumped into the side of a man whose flat-cap leaked white tufts of hair down the sides of his head. He swore and Tabatha felt herself flush and knew her makeup wouldn't hide it.

The woman behind the cash-desk anxiously raised a hand to her blue-rinse as Tabatha approached. The woman's eyes darted between Tabatha's dress, her heels, her bracelets – anywhere but her eyes.

"That's five pounds," she said quickly.

Five pounds, Tabatha thought, *for something so beautiful?* These were so unlike her normal thoughts she barely even heard them, although the word *beautiful* seemed to echo in her mind never entirely fading. But Tabatha was distracted by more prosaic concerns – this dreary little place wouldn't take a credit card would it? Did she have any actual *cash* on her – Tabatha very rarely did. She rummaged through her purse, found a curled up ten pound note and a fifty. Tabatha didn't know if the ten pound note might still have traces of white powder on it, so she absently slapped down the fifty.

There was a pause while the woman stared at the note but didn't touch it.

"We don't take fifty pound notes," she said eventually, gesturing behind her to a photocopied note explaining about forgeries. Tabatha knew everyone in the shop was listening, and even though the woman had spoken meekly she felt both haughty and humiliated. She longed to sweep out but one glance at the mirror stopped her. Angrily, she snatched back the fifty and put the ten pound note down; it curled back up into a tube of its own accord.

"Keep the change!" Tabatha said petulantly, turning away from the woman's look of doubt to struggle with the mirror. Someone held the door open for her, and her nose crinkled with distaste at his smell as she struggled outside. The mirror was hers.

She felt her elation drain from her, a physical falling away of the excitement that had driven her to act so uncharacteristically. She no longer had thoughts that seemed almost those of another (*so beautiful*...) This dissatisfaction with things newly purchased wasn't an uncommon feeling for Tabatha, but it wasn't normally so sudden or as total as this. She looked at the mirror and it seemed so ugly and common that she almost left it on the street where it belonged. But the thought of what her dad might say stopped her, and she lugged it back to the car, where her father was being yelled at by an angry bus driver. On the drive back she sat with it facing away from her, feeling a hatred as it pressed against her legs and threatened to snag her tights. She looked at her reflection in the tinted window, not turning towards her daddy's angry words. Maybe she would burn it or smash the glass when got home. But something lingering within stopped her, and instead she stood it in the place she had planned. Because it was quite an out of the way place in her vast bedchamber it was three days before Tabatha bothered to look in her new mirror for the first time.

~

When she did it wasn't in the best of conditions; a hangover was throbbing behind her temples and squatting heavily in her stomach. Her left tit ached from where it had been groped by that stupid little prick (but crucially a stupid little *rich* prick, from the right sort of family). Her eyelids were at half-mast and she had a terrible urge to cough. It was 2pm.

The mirror was large, raised off the ground on strong wooden legs. It had the proportions of an eye, flipped ninety degrees, two feet high. The frame was unadorned wood, varnish flecking away like dead skin. Despite its lack of sophistication or adornment it had somehow contrived to keep catching Tabatha's eye in the last few days when she had been trying to forget about it. That afternoon she was barely awake before she found herself sitting before it.

Tabatha dared to open her eyes and saw blood red spider webs in the corners, sleep-bruises below. Her nostrils were an ugly red, her skin puffy, her hair crazed. *Bitch,* she thought – whether at herself for looking like she did or at the mirror for daring to show it she didn't know. *Bitch,* almost at the moment the reflection in the mirror changed.

There was a shimmering on the mirror's surface, and seemingly below it too, as if its reflections were three-dimensional. The glittering light spread, brightened, causing Tabatha to cry out, shield her eyes... When she looked back the mirror was clear again, but Tabatha was no longer reflected, and the room it showed was not the one around her.

The image on the surface of the mirror showed a cramped attic room, the ceiling sloped at a violent angle. There was a small window the size of a postage stamp and with glass as dirty as the shadows around it. A bed was slumped against one wall, and next to it was a rickety table piled precariously with books, paper, and CDs. From somewhere in the room ticked a small clock; Tabatha could *hear* it through the mirror, in time with her own heartbeat.

Tabatha went through roughly the same emotions as most would in a similar situation: slow-blinking disbelief, heart-to-throat realisation, dry mouthed nervousness and excitement. (If she missed out anything it was only child-like wonder.)

Yet as she stared into the mirror and saw nothing change, her feelings retreated before her all-powerful hangover. So she had a mirror that showed some crummy attic room instead of her own – great. Maybe the mirror was magic, maybe it had awakened latent psychic powers within her, maybe whatever. But who *cared* if all it showed was an empty bedroom? Certainly not Tabatha with her head threatening to explode or – even worse – keep pounding. She turned away from the mirror, took some painkillers that sat like chalky lead in her stomach. Then she crawled back into bed and fell asleep, with the clock still ticking through the mirror...

...and then she dreamt another's dream. She was a little girl, dressed in red, sitting on a seesaw. But her end of the seesaw remained on the ground because seething dwarves with glowering eyes were holding her down. And above, on the other end of the seesaw, she saw an ugly sister, smirking from her high perch. Anger and frustration burnt within her but she couldn't escape the dwarves' grubby hands.

Yet all the while a voice in her head repeated, You shall *go to the ball; you* shall...

...Tabatha awoke not understanding the words; although they were familiar to her she couldn't place them. She'd been read few fairy tales as a child – what use had she for their stories? *She* already was a beautiful princess, one who already had a goose that laid her golden eggs and protected her from big bad wolves. She had little demand for any fiction, whether on paper or screen. Yet she did have a need for a kind of escapism; even she with her charmed life sought escape and wanted to hear strange stories of others, alluring and addictive.

She felt slightly better now, but also slightly drained, slightly wishy-washy. Her breast still ached – she was glad she hadn't slept with that idiot. Still, his groping and desperately poor kisses would provide Tabatha with more valuable gossip, something for her to talk about with her girlfriends.

Tabatha showered for a long time, feeling her body

rejuvenate in the steam and exotic, bottled aromas. She pulled on a silk dressing gown and brushed her hair in front of the mirror in her en suite. Her reflection looked pleased but slightly rueful – she must still have been drunk, when she'd first awoke, to have imagined what she had! It had just been the aftermath of the party – there was no reason to avoid that charity shop mirror. She purposely got up and went over to sit in front of it.

She was so convinced that it had been her imagination earlier that she'd already half raised her brush to her hair before she realised that it wasn't so. The attic room was still reflected in Tabatha's mirror, and now there was someone in it.

The person was sitting on the bed, her face insubstantially pale save for a firm redness under the eyes. She had obviously been crying and kept glancing at something out of Tabatha's sight with agitation. The trembles of her hands echoed up her arms and shook her slim shoulders. It was obvious she was terrified – and the girl looked exactly like Tabatha.

Well, not exactly. Her blonde hair was dirtier, more stubborn and unstyled. Her eyebrows were larger from being unplucked, her nails were unpainted and bitten ragged. She was wearing a red and white checked uniform, the dress of some cashier or shelf-stacker. But despite these differences the girl did look like Tabatha, they had manifestly the same form and features.

As Tabatha looked on in amazement (closer to child-like wonder this time, but still not there) she heard footsteps approaching. Not from within her room, but from inside the mirror. And from the same source a voice yelled, "*Tabatha!*" and the mirror-girl cringed and locked her fingers together.

There was the sound of a door opening and a triangle of light stabbed into the room. In the middle of the triangle was a giant's shadow, an adult's shadow, a man's shadow, with folded arms and a thick neck sunk into bunched shoulders. The girl looked towards the shadow with obvious fear, but with barely hidden contempt too.

"How much did you get?" the shadow's voice said. The girl bit her lip and reached into the pocket of her uniform. She pulled out some money and held it out to the shadow like an offering. Tabatha couldn't see properly but it looked like a trifling amount. The shadow remained still.

"Is that all?" it said angrily. The mirror-girl replied quickly.

"They haven't offered me much overtime this week! I did all I could but..." She was cut off.

"How is that going to help me and your mother cope? How is *that* going to pay for all the food and clothes and electricity you fuckin' waste?"

The shadow stepped forward into Tabatha's view, revealing itself to be human after all. It was little conciliation, for this human was tall and barrel wide, muscles jostling eagerly in thick arms. He snatched the money from the girl's dwarfed hand and thrust it away into his jeans.

"What fuckin' use is that?" he continued, the cables in his neck knotting. "You bloody suck me dry you do, the amount you take and the amount you give. And you still think you can go to university!" His laughter was full of spite and Tabatha, watching avidly, started to suspect he was drunk.

The mirror-girl looked up at this words, and there was a new, angry eagerness in her voice.

"I *could* go. I'd get a loan, I could apply for..."

The man slapped her with the back of his hand, a lazy, unaimed swipe that still sent the girl sprawling.

"*You're* not going to university", he said, smiling faintly. "You're not going anywhere except to work. I'll call your poncey fuckin' manager and get you more overtime. And you'll do it all, you hear me?"

The girl didn't answer, she was still gingerly touching the split lip he had given her.

"Do you hear me?" the man repeated. "Answer your father!"

"You're not my father!" the girl shrieked, taking Tabatha by surprise. "You might have married Mum but *you are not my father!*" She was enraged, but her rage was eclipsed a second later by the man's shadow, falling over and engulfing her. Tabatha's heart sped up vicariously and her eyes widened as if to take in all the details. She was suddenly acutely aware of the man's large fists and the heavy ring that glinted in the centre of one. The girl was cowering back against the wall, fear diluting her anger and directing it inward, at her own vulnerability.

The man hit the mirror-girl three times, two unhurried blows to the stomach, then a backhand to the face. The girl screamed then moaned, but didn't resist in any way.

"You'll do it all," the man said to her sprawled body. "And bring your father *every* penny. Won't you?"

"Yes." The voice was muffled by the pillow the girl was crying into.

"Yes what?"

"Yes... Dad."

The man laughed, his face primitively satisfied. He left and his shadow evaporated from the room, leaving the mirror-girl curled up on the bed. She was crying but trying not to, for her sobs hurt her belly.

Eventually the girl's weeping grew less intense and blubbery, and she sat up and blew her hair out of her face. Her eyes were bright, evaporating wet pain into an arid anger. She was now hunched forward like a chess player over the board, scheming.

But her eyes gradually dimmed and pooled with reality; her concentration drained out of her with a sigh that deflated her head into her hands. After a while she got up with an awkward wince and walked away out of Tabatha's sight.

When she returned her hair was wet and she had a towel wrapped round her body. This dropped to the floor and for half a minute Tabatha saw the green, blue, and grey jewellery that adorned the mirror-girl's body, the presents her step-father had given her. The girl pulled on cheap underwear, blue jeans, and a white T-shirt with fraying stitching at one shoulder. Then the girl picked up a hairbrush and suddenly thrust her face right up to Tabatha's, causing Tabatha to jerk away from the mirror in alarm. But it became obvious that the girl couldn't see her, she was merely brushing her hair in her own mirror, which by an odd coincidence (nothing more surely?) happened to be in the spot Tabatha was watching from.

Tabatha studied the mirror-girl's face, thankful for and delighted by all the differences. It was redder, slightly plumper, not as smooth or well looked after – but it was undeniably hers. It was like looking into a distorting mirror at a funfair. *One that's turned me into an ugly commoner!* Tabatha thought smugly.

After spending an unusually short amount of time doing her hair the mirror-girl sat down on her bed, lifted her pillow like the lid to a treasure chest, and pulled out a small ring-bound notebook, creased and dog eared. She leant over this with a similar but less hateful intensity than before, and started writing... When she was finished she hid the book back under her pillow, and turned on some music and lay back on her bed reading.

Later she went on to do other things. Tabatha watched her the whole time.

~

Tabatha's nights were generally busy: either the stuffiness of social engagements with her family's friends, or the frantic, fashionably debauched parties of her peers. Conversely her days tended to be quite, quite bland. Much time was spent shopping, or in spas, or simply in bed waiting for the hangover to abate. The rest of the long, sunlit hours she spent moping, pacing her room, flicking aimlessly through the latest magazines or watching patronising, lowest-common-denominator TV. She ignored the soaps, the quiz programmes, the endless cop shows. What she liked to watch were the fly on the wall documentaries, the reality TV, the CCTV footage of down and outs and the commonplace. She watched these shows intently, hunched forward, as if they were documenting the lives of strange tribes in impenetrable forests.

So the mirror... the mirror was a veritable wish come true for Tabatha, an unfolding lowlife documentary just for her, 24 hours a day! Tabatha had always been amazed that the lower classes, the real dregs of society, didn't take one look at their situation and run, lemming-like, straight off Beachy Head. Tabatha knew she would absolutely die in their situation. To have to live in a mouldy little shoebox of a house, to have to wear ill-fitting and no doubt itchy clothes. To have grime on your skin, and a job that put folds in your face and creases in your spine – and be paid a pittance for it!

And the mirror-girl (Tabatha refused to call her Tabatha) was in an even worse and fascinating situation. Watching her for the last few days, Tabatha had seen the girl beaten twice more by her stepfather, although not as severely as the first time. The girl handed over money to him, with which he bought alcohol as soon as he could (Tabatha could actually smell the whisky on his breath *through* the mirror, when he stooped close enough under the low eaves.) She'd seen the mother once, black-eyed and pale – Tabatha had dismissed her instantly as being too weak-willed and passive to be a major player in the drama she was watching.

After being beaten the mirror-girl sat drawn together in ferocious anger, an arch-plotter with no viable plans for revenge or escape. Her anger always faded with nothing having changed. And in this apathetic aftermath the girl would read, or listen to appalling music, or write what seemed to be poetry, as far as Tabatha could tell. It seemed out of character for such a girl, but she thought that was all it could be, albeit pointless and absurd.

The mirror-girl irritated Tabatha immensely but she still couldn't stop herself watching her. She stared raptly into the mirror when she had nothing else to do, and found herself still watching hours later when she should have been getting ready to go out. She was displeased when the mirror-girl wasn't visible, and at those times she wondered about the girl's life: where were her friends, her extended family, her dates? How had her tyrannical stepfather isolated her so? Would the girl always cower in her room, returning from work to do nothing but read and listen to music and write poetry that was no doubt as poor as she was? Or would she stand-up to her stepfather or run away? (Tabatha hoped not!) Maybe she would get him arrested, form a conspiracy with her secret boyfriend, the spotty son of a butcher or someone, and murder her oppressor somehow – poison or a quick blow to the head... Exciting stuff.

Tabatha had long since got used to the magic of her mirror. It was no different to her 3D TV or her touch-screen tablet – just another fancy toy that someone like her no doubt deserved. It was only right and fitting that if there were such things as enchanted mirrors she should own at least one. But whichever power decided these things obviously didn't do so on the basis of wealth or social standing. For the one day Tabatha saw the girl drag into her attic room an almost identical mirror to hers, its deformed twin.

It wasn't exactly the same, the most obvious difference being that it had no legs to stand on, although there was some picture wire attached to its back to allow it to be hung. Apart from that it was near enough identical, a few extra scars and scratches, but that was all. The mirror-girl was gazing at it disappointedly, and Tabatha knew with a sudden spark of empathy the girl had been coming home from work, seen the mirror in a shop or junk heap and felt she just *had* to have it. And after handing over the money she had felt her elation drain, but dragged the thing home anyway... Tabatha peered at the scene in front of her more intently. Now this *was* interesting...

The girl starred at her new mirror despondently, then moved out of sight to turn on some music. It was all just noise and Northern vowel sounds to Tabatha – she wouldn't have recognised *Breaking Into Heaven* from any of the parties that she went to. The girl seemed to cheer herself up by singing along to the opening lines; Tabatha guessed the girl's stepfather wasn't in, he normally yelled at her if she made any noise.

Dragging the mirror the girl walked almost right up to the spot Tabatha observed her from; again the girl's face was close up and level with her own. Tabatha saw a small ladybird of acne on the girl's forehead and grimaced with disgust. Couldn't these people even wash properly?

The girl reached up and took down her old mirror – a small pound shop kind of thing. She put it into a drawer, evidently not one to throw anything away. Then the girl identical to Tabatha picked up the mirror identical to

Tabatha's – it was obviously intended as a replacement. A sliver of intuition pierced Tabatha's thoughts; she felt distinctly uneasy, although she couldn't have said why.

The girl hefted up the mirror, the back of it entirely filling Tabatha's view; all she could see was raw wood with a scrawl of illegible charcoal in one corner. The girl was still singing, but under her breath now, unthinkingly. The wood moved as the girl tried to find the nail, then there was clink to indicate she had. The back of the mirror shifted a few millimetres to the perfect position and then...

Then a bright light filled Tabatha's vision, like a giant welding torch burning through the mirror. She heard the girl on the other side cry out...

...Tabatha cried out and looked away from the mirror, from which light was cascading out. What the hell..? she thought. There had been something weird about the mirror from the start when it had seemed to call to her. Not even the thought of what her stepfather would say or do had deterred her. She'd regretted it the instant she'd had the mirror in her possession, but she wasn't one to throw anything away.

The light quickly faded, leaving bright afterimages dancing in Tabatha's eyes. She blinked rapidly and looked back at the mirror. She gasped – the background behind her was not her room! She raised a hand to her mouth, and noticed that her reflection didn't. She peered closer and saw the powder on her reflection's cheeks, the sheen of her shorter hair, the plucked brows and thick lashes framing older looking eyes. Tabatha didn't know whether to feel afraid or amazed. She looked at the girl in the mirror and their eyes met...

...the mirror-girl started at Tabatha and their eyes met. Both their mouths dropped open and four eyebrows lifted; for a moment it was as if they really were reflections of another. Then the mirror-girl hesitantly spoke.

"H... hello?" she said, sounding very young.

"Hello," Tabatha said warily. For a second she had an urge to smash the mirror, to forget all about it and the doppelganger on the other side... But she couldn't do that, couldn't destroy her new toy; her crystal ball. But still, she felt afraid and couldn't think why. Despite the bizarre situation there was surely nothing here that could harm her, was there?

"Are you real?" the mirror-girl asked wonderingly, almost vacantly.

"Of course I'm real!" snapped Tabatha. The girl looked briefly startled, her eyes widened again.

"S... sorry," she mumbled, then more hopefully "I'm real too!" She laughed brightly, but it quickly changed into the kind of laughter that was only there to fill the silence when other people should have been laughing, but weren't. Tabatha forced a smile just to make her stop.

"It's hard to know what to say isn't it?" the mirror-girl said. "Nothing like this has ever happened to me before! It's like something out of a book isn't it? *Alice Through The Looking Glass* or something?"

"I suppose so," Tabatha said. The worried feeling had not gone away. In fact there was something in what the girl had just said that worried her even more, but she wasn't quite sure what. It hovered outside her conscious grasp, something threatening.

She started and realised the girl was still talking.

"Wh...what?"

"I was just wondering how this thing works. How is it *happening?*"

Tabatha shrugged.

"I guess it's not important. I guess what's important is that it *is* happening, not how."

There was a sound from the other side of the mirror (or whatever it was now it had joined with its twin), the sound of a door slamming, which Tabatha barely noticed. But the mirror girl's head whipped round, and when she looked back at Tabatha her eyes had rabbit-widened with fear.

"My stepfather's back! He'll kill me when he sees I've bought this mirror!"

Tabatha didn't know what to say; what *was* there to say? The mirror-girl was going to get beaten, probably severely this time; no words of Tabatha's could help, nor would it help if Tabatha didn't watch it happen... She resisted the urge to shrug again. The mirror-girl looked round her room as if seeking an escape, a bolt-hole.

Then she paused, as if listening to something. She looked back at the mirror with hazy, obedient eyes.

Tabatha felt another, sharper stab of premonition. She suddenly knew what it was that the girl had said that had worried her so much. *Alice Through The Looking Glass*...

The mirror girl also seemed to have had some sudden knowledge bloom in her, for she reached out to touch the mirror's surface confidently, almost lazily...

"No!" Tabatha shouted. (Through. The scary word was *through*.) Surely what she feared couldn't be about to happen? She liked watching her in her soap-opera world, but surely this commoner couldn't travel through the mirror? Into Tabatha's own world, into *her* room...

The girl was still humming the song, even thought the music was no longer playing.

Her hand touched the glass and for a split-second Tabatha saw her palm pressed white. Then, as before, a great light filled the mirror, a world changing brilliance...

...Tabatha's hand touched the mirror and for a split second it felt like it was pulsing. Then, like before, the whole mirror boiled over with a light that seemed to stop the world from turning. Tabatha felt a pulling sensation, a sucking vortex distorted her face and pulled her hair up into a unicorn's horn. Her feet lifted from the ground. Her head was pinpricked by a hundred pains as her hair strained upwards. Some of her hairs were pulled out of her head; these loose hairs fell casually to the ground as if the force clutching at Tabatha no longer cared about them now they weren't a part of her, now they had already started to die...

Then the crown of Tabatha's head touched the mirror's whirlpool of light; more and more of her was dragged upwards and into the mirror... and then her head was through, her face was through and she saw...

...saw the mirror-girl's head emerge from the shimmering turbulence of the mirror and Tabatha felt a wave of distaste and anger. This wasn't supposed to happen! This girl, this pleb, wasn't allowed in *her* room! But she was coming, with her grease and germs, her aches and acne and wretched stories. Tabatha placed both hands on the girl's face and tried to push her backwards to where she belonged. The girl cried out, tried to turn her head aside, but Tabatha had already realised the force pushing her forwards was far stronger than she was. She stood back and wiped her hands on her dressing gown. The mirror-girl's shoulders emerged, then her arms were free and reaching, and Tabatha stepped back another step in horrified fury. She watched as the girl was thrust out of the claustrophobic womb of her own world, born beneath the spread and wooden-stirruped legs of Tabatha's mirror onto the pale carpet below.

The girl lay gasping like a fish out of water – but not for long. She stood on trembling legs, exertion birthmarks fading from her face.

"Why did you try and push me *back?*" was the first thing she said, both fists pressed to her hips.

"I... I was... scared," Tabatha said, truthfully enough. She was trying not to show her anger, and had one hand still pressed to her quivering lips. Her answer seemed to satisfy the mirror-girl, who breathed out deeply and looked at the room around her, taking in the double bed, the walk in wardrobe, the open door to the en suite... She seemed oddly comfortable and composed, which Tabatha didn't think was right. The *girl* should feel nervous and out of place; so why was it Tabatha herself who felt that way?

"Wow," the girl said, her head craning upwards. "You live here? This is your *bedroom?*"

Tabatha tried to reply but could only cough, her wary affirmative caught in one cupped hand.

"Fucking hell," the girl said softly. "Your parents must

be really posh. I mean... sorry..." She smiled again. "But what do they *do?*"

Tabatha found herself unable to reply again – what *did* her parents do? How did they provide for her? She didn't actually know.

"It's none of your business," she said finally.

"Fair enough," the mirror-girl said, "sure." She walked over to the bay windows, which looked out over the grounds; she leant forward like a child seeing snow for the first time. "But... wow. Do your parents *own* all of this?"

"S...some of it," Tabatha said self-consciously. She didn't know why she couldn't assert herself, why she was being drowned out. It just felt impossible, like trying to make conversation with a burglar who was ransacking your home.

"You must walk around it all the time..." the girl murmured, still looking out the window. "I could lose myself for hours, just wandering..." She tore herself from the outstretching view and walked around the rest of the room, her eyes widening to absorb it all. She didn't even look towards the seething Tabatha, banished in a corner. *I will handle this myself*, Tabatha thought, *I will not call my father*. Her painted nails dug into her palms as she tried to think of something adequate to say.

"Can't really wander around where *I* live," the girl continued, briefly glancing at Tabatha but really talking to herself. "Not in those streets. Hard to get inspiration *there*. I mean..." She seemed briefly embarrassed. "I mean, for writing. I try and write stories, and you know, sometimes poems. I don't normally tell... can't tell my stepfather obviously. And how do you tell your mates without sounding like a twat? I bet *you* think that, but I guess because you're like me I thought... I mean... I don't know you but you *look* like me so I thought if I told you..."

"*I don't care!*" Tabatha suddenly yelled. She stamped her foot but it was inaudible on the thick carpet. Her face was blood-red and twisted. What did *stories* have to do with all of this?

"Wh...what?" the girl said, off balance. Tabatha felt furious.

"You can't... You can't be here!"

"But I *am*."

"I mean..." Tabatha spluttered, and wiped spittle from her lips with her silk sleeve. "This is *my* room, *my* house! You have to go back!"

"I don't think I can," the girl said with alarming confidence.

"What? Why?" Tabatha demanded. Event to herself she sounded like a child. She felt like she could hear someone laughing in her head. It wasn't fair!

The girl reached out and touched the mirror, first with her fingertips, then with the flat of her hand. Nothing happened, no light engulfed her. When she removed her hand a sweaty palm print slowly faded, evidence disappearing from the scene of a crime.

"One way ticket," the girl murmured.

Her action made both girls look back at the mirror itself and its view of a faraway attic room. The stepfather could be seen prowling around the miniature high room, like an ogre looking for a princess. Stooped under the eaves of the room he looked hunched and furious; he was clutching a bottle of whisky like a club.

"You think I want to go back there?" the girl said vaguely, to someone.

"But...But it's where you belong!" Tabatha said.

"*Belong?*" The girl turned to Tabatha, and her eyes were bitter above her suddenly flushed and blazing cheeks. "Belong? Why the fuck should *anyone* belong there?"

"Well you don't belong *here!*" Tabatha said, desperately angry, sure something vital was at stake but not knowing what. "*I* belong here! Not you – look at you! Your clothes, your accent, your cheapness... You can't belong here!"

The mirror-girl's face hardened; whereas before she had seemed younger than her years she now seemed older. When she laughed it was bitter.

"Why did you have to say that? Why did you? I mean, I could tell as soon as I saw you that you were better off than me. And when I saw this room... But we've got something wonderful here! A magic mirror, like from a fairy story! And you have to bring *class and wealth* into it? Can't you just..." She sighed, looked down, seemed to shrink. "Oh I don't know. Just... I don't know."

"But..." Tabatha said – never before had so much scorn been directed at her, it confused and enraged her. She couldn't find the obvious response she knew must exist, to put the mirror-girl in her place. "You don't belong here," she repeated. "You just *don't.* What would you do here?"

"What do *you* do here?" the girl shot back.

"H... how dare... I... *look...*"

"We could have great fun together," the girl said

imploringly, searching Tabatha's face for something. "The two of us looking the same, think about it! Having an identical double..."

"You are not my double!" Tabatha yelled, scarlet mapping itself across her face. The girl flinched and seemed to lose some of her confidence. She stared at Tabatha as if to check what she had said.

"What do you mean? We look the same."

Tabatha gritted her teeth, but knew it wasn't going to hold back what she had to say. But within the core of her surely justifiable anger was a heavy cold ball of fear, which her anger couldn't melt or her bile eat away.

"You *don't* look the same as me! Your... Your hair's all greasy and horrible – did you cut it yourself? What about your spots and that T-shirt falling apart? And, and your skin's all dry, you're fatter than me..."

"I could look like you!" the mirror-girl said, all serenity vanished now. Like Tabatha her face had turned blood-coloured with anger. "I could look like you if I was rich and had fancy makeup and fucking face-packs and... with all your jewels and clothes and everything! If I didn't have to work like you, if my stepfather didn't... I could be beautiful too!" She stopped, seemingly embarrassed by the childish word, then decided she didn't care: "I could be beautiful too!"

"Oh yeah?" Tabatha sneered. She was horrified by how ineloquent (how *common*...) the words made her sound, but her emotions had unarticulated her.

"Yes," said the girl defiantly. "I can prove it."

Tabatha didn't want to ask, but pride made her, the desire to win the argument and shut the girl up made her.

"How?" she said suspiciously, and her reflection told her.

~

Later, two girls stood and looked at each other in a bedroom so large it might have been in a palace. They stood before a magic mirror, a refugee from a fairy tale. Maybe this mirror had seen it all – seen a princess rescued from high entrapment, seen an ugly duckling turn into a white swan, seen many a wicked witch or ugly sister punished, seen many a glass slipper fit a serving girl's foot, and many a happy ever after...

The mirror, or something within, watched.

~

The girl examined herself in the mirror and smiled – a pearl-like smile which obviously wasn't intended to humiliate Tabatha. But it did. The mirror-girl was wearing Tabatha's clothes, right down to the underwear. She had powdered her face, washed her hair, painted her nails, all in the privacy of Tabatha's en suite. The dress she had picked out of the walk-in wardrobe seemed to have been made for her, its colour complimenting her eyes and its folds and curves fitting her just right. High white shoes made her seem taller and more confident. The glitter of jewellery was discreet but becoming. The mirror-girl twirled and so did her reflection – she looked gorgeous and she knew it.

Tabatha knew it too. She couldn't help the irritation she felt twisting her face into an ugly shape. Without makeup, her face felt hot and unclean, her entire body felt itchy under the cotton and cheap denim of the mirror-girl's clothes. The dirty trainers bit into Tabatha's feet. She had removed all her jewellery, even ruffed up her hair. Everything felt odd, dreamlike but too intense at the same time. She was uncomfortably aware of her body's every movement as it chafed against the unfamiliar clothing, of every breath and beat of her heart strong then weakening in her limbs. Taunting voices sang in her head; she felt like she was somehow being watched and judged.

Again Tabatha relied on anger from her almost limitless account to counter these feelings. It rose and coiled in her, not entirely under her control. It curled her fingers and snarled her face. It exploded thoughts in her head like Devil-bangers: so what if the girl looked more attractive (*so beautiful...*) now? Of course she did – didn't she have on *Tabatha's* dress, *Tabatha's* necklace and perfume? But what was more important to Tabatha, what had come to symbolise so much more, was what she looked like in the mirror-girl's clothes. Surely she still looked beautiful, would always do so no matter what rags she was wearing? *That* was what mattered and what would show the differences between them. Tabatha rudely gestured the other girl away and stood in front of the mirror herself.

She found it odd how the mirror was suddenly reflecting her room again, and not showing the world the mirror-girl had come from. *It's as if it's got a mind of its own...* she thought, before all such thoughts were driven from her head. Her reflection caught her reaction to how she looked, and scowled.

She still looked good, the average man passing in the average street might still have swung his gaze over her, might still have let her figure linger pleasantly in his thoughts for a few seconds. But stunningly beautiful she was not. Tabatha's roving, over-critical eye noticed many things: black crescents under her eyes without makeup to hide them, vague and undefined looking lips, the beginning of a spot clear against her too pale skin. The white T-shirt hung limply from her, her breasts seemed smaller and oddly shaped in whatever the mirror-girl was wearing for a bra. It wasn't just the clothes – she looked uncomfortable in her own body, and completely out of place in the rich, lavish room around her.

Where she looked like she belonged was in her own worst nightmare: in a chicken-coop terrace or tower block flat, choosing between call-centres or the dole queue, and making three wishes every week on the lottery. And meanwhile, half a world away, rich girls like the one behind her paraded around in expensive dresses, waiting for the dalliances of the night... Tabatha felt her sense of self slipping away into the life she had observed only from the outside, losing itself in fifty-nine million souls that were no longer entertaining when seen in extreme close-up, when you were thrust *into* your crystal ball...

"No!" Tabatha shouted, flicking back to reality. It was time to end this ridiculous game, this charade! She knew who she was – she was Tabatha. She knew who she was, where she belonged, what clothes she should be wearing, and it was time to show it to the flea bitten upstart behind her. Her anger writhed and hissed – *she* was the beautiful one! The image in front of her was a lie, another trick from the unpredictable mirror. She would destroy the mirror, be done with it and its lies forever. Then she would demand her clothing back, tell the mirror-girl exactly what she thought of her, get Daddy's driver to throw her out, and then forget all about the episode. She smiled viciously at the girl, her eyes burning with distaste. The ice ball of fear was still present in her stomach, but she knew it would be melted soon.

Tabatha's fists were already clenched, and she swung one at the mirror, telling herself it would definitely be worth a few cuts and seven years bad luck.

When her knuckles were almost there she thought, *Wait, what if...*, but by then it was too late. Something laughed, both inside her head and outside all she knew.

Then her hand touched the skin of the mirror, felt it squirm and suck. Intense light blinded her and her head was pulled forward, her hair wind-tunnelled around her face...

...Tabatha saw the mirror-girl's hair obscure her face, which was drawn into the sucking maw of the mirror. The girl had time for one scream before it was cut off. Her feet left the plush carpet and kicked in midair. Tabatha felt both sympathy and satisfaction, fear and wonder. Soon all of the mirror-girl has been sucked inside, save for one of the cheap trainers she had been wearing, which fell to the floor. There was a smacking sound and all the light cascaded in on itself, falling back into what had made it. Then the mirror exploded, thousands of shards of glass spraying out across the room like jewellery. A great power, a great presence, seemed to leave the room.

Tabatha stood stock-still for a few seconds, then she picked up the trainer and stared at it thoughtfully. Hints of some memory, some dream, lapped tantalisingly at her thoughts then retreated out of reach, content to have raised goose bumps from her flesh. You shall...

Eventually Tabatha, ever the dutiful daughter, the servant girl, cleared up all the glass, wrapping it safely in one of the mirror-girl's society magazines. Then she stood quietly and wondered what to do. She looked at the expensive dresses in the wardrobe, the girl's dreadful music collection, the view of greenery outside the bay windows. Beyond the woods and fields she thought she could see a faint grey smudge of industry or housing – she strained her eyes but couldn't be sure. Maybe it was a place like where she had come from; maybe it was where she had come from. Whatever, she was glad it was just visible, so that she wouldn't forget it existed, that it was real.

Sometime later she opened the door of the bedroom, to see what she would find. Her mind was full of hopes and fears, ideas and worries. She shut the door behind her. And then she...

...Tabatha fell and sprawled on the bare floorboards, dust choking her throat. There was a sound like some giant smacking its lips together in satisfaction, and then a thousand daggers of glass sprayed all over her, rattling on the floor and stinging her through her market-stall T-shirt. A voice identical to hers said, "*One way ticket...*"

Tabatha got up, and banged her head on the low sloping ceiling of the attic room. This place is ridiculous! she thought angrily. Then she jumped in alarm as a booming voice called,

"*Tabatha?* Where are you? Where the *fuck* have you been? *What was that noise?*"

No sound escaped Tabatha's swollen throat. She ran to the now empty frame of the mirror, begging inside her head. But it was no use, nothing existed in this world to grant her wishes. She looked around the rabbit hutch-sized room as she heard heavy, angry footsteps start to climb the stairs – the sound of an approaching troll, a big bad wolf, an evil stepfather. Tabatha whimpered, thrust her knuckles into her mouth. How could this be happening to her? She clutched at the mirror again, but even its frame was now cracked, and it fell from the nail and hit the floor. Tabatha stared at it and tears sprang from her eyes.

The door slammed open and shook the whole room. A shadow stepped forward into the light, bulging with drunken malevolence.

"*Where have you been?*" the stepfather bellowed, the smell of whisky radiating from him. Tabatha tried to speak but only babbled.

"And what's all this fuckin' glass doing everywhere?"

"Now look," Tabatha managed, "this isn't what you think..."

"What the *fuck's* with that snooty voice? Is that any way to speak to your father?"

"You are *not* my father!"

The shadow stepped forward, its hands clenched and raised and mallet-like. The stepfather's face was bursting with crimson, scarred with rage.

"You spend money – money you owe me! – on a mirror and then you *smash* it? You put on a posh voice and then...? Fucking hell girl, you need to be taught a lesson by your Dad, a very harsh fuckin' lesson!"

He came towards her, as inexorable as something from a horror story. Tabatha backed away but there was nowhere to go. Tears blurred her vision; she heard whirling laughter as her spine scraped the wall. She was still trying to speak – to protest that this wasn't right, that this wasn't *her* – when she saw the first punch coming, the gold ring she would come to know so well gleaming in the centre of it. And embedded in the ring was a small jewel and Tabatha saw her reflection, small and terrified, and the prism of the jewel split the image, showing it happening many, many times, because this was *her* story now...

Now, and ever after.

gary mcmahon is the author of several novels, including the Thomas Usher books and The Concrete Grove trilogy. His acclaimed short fiction has been reprinted in various Year's Best anthologies. He lives and works in Yorkshire, where he practices shotokan karate, tries to be a good husband and father, and sifts through the minutiae of modern life so he can turn what he finds into stories.

His website can be found at **garymcmahon.com**

sean t page is a zombie survival expert and has provided consultancy to private industry and governments around the world on what to do in the event of a zombie apocalypse. Admittedly, few of them actually asked for the advice in the first place.

His qualifications include a 25-metre swimming badge from school and several merits for good attendance. He launched the Ministry of Zombies in 2009 to raise awareness of the zombie threat and has published some books.

You can follow his varied adventures at **crazyadventuresincybersecurity.com**. Don't be put off by the title, there's an emphasis on crazy in the blog.

jasper bark is infectious - and there's no known cure. If you're reading this then you're already at risk of contamination. The symptoms will begin to manifest any moment now. There's nothing you can do about it. There's no itching or unfortunate rashes, but you'll become obsessed with his books, from the award winning collections *Dead Air* and *Stuck on You and Other*

Prime Cuts, to cult novels like *The Final Cut* and acclaimed graphic novels such as *Bloodfellas* and *Beyond Lovecraft*. Soon you'll want to tweet, post and blog about his work until thousands of others fall under its viral spell. We're afraid there's no way to avoid this, these words contain a power you are hopeless to resist. You're already in their thrall and have been since you started this book. Even now you find yourself itching to read the rest of his work. Don't fight it, embrace the urge and wear your affliction with pride!

Trust your Uncle Jasp on this, you know it makes sense.

lily childs has an obsession with misunderstood demons and takes unsavoury delight in Victorian underworlds, twisted myths and the necrotic. Her warped fairy tale *In Search of Silver Boughs* follows Emmeline, Augustus and Ishtabelle in their traumatic journey through Europe across the centuries, all the way to the frozen Thames.

Lily's dark horror, crime and ghost stories have been published by KnightWatch Press, Crystal Lake Publishing, The Sinister Horror Company, Ganglion Press, Western Legends Publishing and James Ward Kirk Fiction. She has recently completed a supernatural asylum novel. A second gallows novel hangs in the balance.

james everington mainly writes dark, supernatural fiction, although he occasionally takes a break and writes dark, non-supernatural fiction. His second collection of such tales, *Falling Over*, is out now from Infinity Plus.

He's also the author of *The Quarantined City*, an episodic novel mixing Borgesian strangeness with supernatural horror – "an unsettling voice all of its own" *The Guardian* – and the novellas *Paupers' Graves* and *Trying To Be So Quiet*.

Alongside Dan Howarth, he has co-edited the anthologies *The Hyde Hotel* (Black Shuck Books) and *Imposter Syndrome* (Dark Minds Press).

Oh, and he drinks Guinness, if anyone's asking. You can find out what James is currently up to at his Scattershot Writing site –

jameseverington.blogspot.co.uk